S0-BDH-139

Joshua stopped and looked down at Riley

The glow from the streetlights barely touched her features. The cold seeped into Joshua's skin, and he realized he'd forgotten his gloves. "I guess this wasn't such a good idea," he admitted.

"I don't care about the cold," Riley said. But *he* did.

With no other choice, he reached for her hand and put it in his left pocket. Now, with her fingers curled around his, Riley was closer to him than she'd ever been, probably ever would be.

As they walked, Joshua could feel her hold on him, her slender fingers entwined with his, and he was less cold than he'd been a moment ago.

Things had suddenly got a whole lot more complicated. He realized that he'd been desperate to touch her before, and right now he never wanted to let go.

Dear Reader,

Judging Joshua is the second book in my RETURN TO SILVER CREEK series. Joshua Pierce goes back to Silver Creek, Nevada, with a broken heart and the knowledge that he has loved and loved well, but he'll never love again. He and his small daughter have returned to the mountain to help his sick father. When he makes an arrest on a winding snowy road, he doesn't yet know that not only will his heart heal, he'll find love can come a second time and make his life whole again.

Riley Shaw has never loved and truly feels that love is for others, not for her. When she's arrested just outside the town of Silver Creek, she's certain that life can't get any worse. What she doesn't know is that when Joshua Pierce comes into her life, everything will change and she'll find out what love is all about.

I hope you enjoy *Judging Joshua* and you'll look for the third book in my RETURN TO SILVER CREEK series.

Mary Anne Wilson

Judging Joshua
Mary Anne Wilson

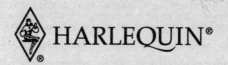

HARLEQUIN®

TORONTO • NEW YORK • LONDON
AMSTERDAM • PARIS • SYDNEY • HAMBURG
STOCKHOLM • ATHENS • TOKYO • MILAN • MADRID
PRAGUE • WARSAW • BUDAPEST • AUCKLAND

If you purchased this book without a cover you should be aware
that this book is stolen property. It was reported as "unsold and
destroyed" to the publisher, and neither the author nor the
publisher has received any payment for this "stripped book."

For Emily Vaughn Geisler
a.k.a. Bunky
Thank you for all the love and joy
you've brought into my life.
Love, Mamaw

ISBN 0-373-75082-X

JUDGING JOSHUA

Copyright © 2005 by Mary Anne Wilson.

All rights reserved. Except for use in any review, the reproduction or
utilization of this work in whole or in part in any form by any electronic,
mechanical or other means, now known or hereafter invented, including
xerography, photocopying and recording, or in any information storage
or retrieval system, is forbidden without the written permission of the
publisher, Harlequin Enterprises Limited, 225 Duncan Mill Road,
Don Mills, Ontario M3B 3K9, Canada.

All characters in this book have no existence outside the imagination of
the author and have no relation whatsoever to anyone bearing the same
name or names. They are not even distantly inspired by any individual
known or unknown to the author, and all incidents are pure invention.

This edition published by arrangement with Harlequin Books S.A.

® and TM are trademarks of the publisher. Trademarks indicated with
® are registered in the United States Patent and Trademark Office, the
Canadian Trade Marks Office and in other countries.

www.eHarlequin.com

Printed in U.S.A.

ABOUT THE AUTHOR

Mary Anne Wilson is a Canadian transplanted to Southern California, where she lives with her husband, three children and an assortment of animals. She knew she wanted to write romances when she found herself "rewriting" the great stories in literature, such as *A Tale of Two Cities*, to give them "happy endings." Over her long career she's published more than thirty romances, had her books on bestseller lists, been nominated for Reviewer's Choice Awards and received a Career Achievement Award in Romantic Suspense. She's looking forward to her next thirty books.

Books by Mary Anne Wilson

HARLEQUIN AMERICAN ROMANCE

*Just for Kids
†Return to Silver Creek

Don't miss any of our special offers. Write to us at the following address for information on our newest releases.

Harlequin Reader Service
U.S.: 3010 Walden Ave., P.O. Box 1325, Buffalo, NY 14269
Canadian: P.O. Box 609, Fort Erie, Ont. L2A 5X3

Chapter One

Going back to Silver Creek should have been a good thing. But going back to his hometown had been hard for Joshua Pierce.

He stepped out of the old stone-and-brick police station on a side street in the town and into the bitter cold of November. The brilliance of the sun glinting off the last snowfall made him narrow his eyes as he finished shrugging into the heavy, green uniform jacket over his jeans and white T-shirt. He didn't bother doing it up as he headed for the closest squad car in the security parking lot at the side of the building.

Easing his six-foot-tall frame into the cruiser, he turned on the motor and flipped the heater on high. He sat there while the warmth gathered. Two months ago he'd been in Atlanta, in the humid heat of September, with no intention of coming home. Then his world shifted, the way it had more than a year earlier, but this time it was his father who'd needed him.

He was back in Silver Creek, without an idea what he'd do when he left here again. And he would leave.

This wasn't home anymore. For now he worked, filling in for his father, while the old man recovered from a heart attack, and getting by day by day. It worked. He made it to the next day, time and time again. And that was enough for him.

He pushed the car into gear, hit the release for the security gate, then drove out onto the side street. Turning north on the main street, he looked off toward the rugged peaks of the Sierra Nevada soaring into the heavy gray sky. Silver Creek had some of the best skiing in the West.

The original section of town looked about the same, with old stone-and-brick buildings, some dating back to the silver strike in the 1800s. They looked like a time warp from the past, until you looked more closely and saw that the feed store was now a high-end ski equipment shop. The general store had been transformed into a trendy coffee bar and a specialty cookie store.

Some buildings were the same. Rusty's Diner was still Rusty's Diner, run by the red-haired man, and the hotel was still the Silver Creek Hotel. But everything else was changing, and even in Silver Creek, change was inevitable. You couldn't fight it, he thought as he drove farther north into the newer section where the stores were unabashedly high-end. He'd tried to fight the changes in his life, but, in the end, he hadn't been able to resist.

He slowed for the influx of traffic at the public skiing slopes to the west and headed away from the bustle of the visitors. Picking up his two-way radio handset, Joshua called in, told them where he was, then settled in for the drive north. He glanced to the west and observed the reason Silver Creek had changed so much in the past ten years. The Inn at Silver Creek.

At first all anyone could see was the high stone wall, partially covered by snow, that seemed to go on forever to the north. It actually ran for two miles before you reached the impressive main entrance. He'd clocked it once for something to do on one of his drives.

The Inn was pricey, fancy, ultraprivate and totally secluded on more than a hundred acres that just happened to encompass the best ski runs in the area. As if thinking of Jack Prescott, the developer and owner of most of Silver Creek, had made him materialize, Joshua approached the front of the inn and spotted Jack's car on the cobbled entryway that led to massive wooden gates. The red Porsche, a horrible car to be driving up here in the snow, was idling by the guard station. Ryce, the guard on duty, glanced up from his conversation with Jack, who looked in Joshua's direction, and both men waved.

Joshua beeped his horn and kept going. He'd see Jack later. They'd talk. They'd have a few drinks. Despite the fact that when they were kids they'd thought they could solve the world's problems, they knew better now. Even if it looked as if the sheriff's kid and the rich kid hadn't had much in common, they had been, and still were, friends.

The boundaries of the town were far-reaching, and Joshua often used the time on his rounds to be alone. But as he drove past the last traces of the stone wall that marked the end of Jack's land, he realized he wasn't going to have the pleasure of peace and quiet, at least not now.

A black luxury car came toward him from the opposite direction, going too fast, sliding into the curve, then catching traction and heading south. It whizzed past him and Joshua knew he couldn't let it go. Not on these roads. He swung a quick U-turn and took off after the car. He clocked it at sixty miles an hour, which was about twenty miles too fast for the road. Pulling up behind it, Joshua flipped on his lights and siren. It took a good ten seconds before the driver reacted and he saw the brake lights flash, noted the sudden slowing before it pulled over.

Joshua pulled in behind the car and called the station. He asked Deputy Wesley Gray to run the plates. He'd been used to better equipment in Atlanta, but things took longer in Silver Creek. Everything took longer in the town. Reaching for his uniform hat, Joshua got out and ducked into the chilled wind as he headed to the car.

As he approached, he noticed the car had heavily tinted windows. A BMW, he noted, Illinois plates, practically brand-new. He thought he could make out one person inside.

At the driver's window, he tapped the glass, and it slid down silently. He bent to look inside. The driver was a woman, but she didn't fit the type he'd expect to be handling such a car. He'd thought the luxury sedan had most likely been heading for the inn, or cutting through on its way to Las Vegas.

But the woman behind the wheel was pretty, even

with the frown of annoyance on her face. Dark hair shot with auburn was pulled back severely in a ponytail from a makeup-free face dominated by deep blue eyes. Long lashes, defined eyebrows, small nose, full lips and an angry look on a slightly pale face. He could see the way her left hand gripped the top of the steering wheel so tightly her knuckles were bloodless. But she didn't have the glitter of gold and diamonds at her fingers, ears or neck.

A plain chambray shirt and jeans weren't even stylishly faded and worn. They were just faded and worn. She didn't fit the car at all. "What's the problem?" she asked abruptly in a breathy voice edged with that anger and annoyance he'd easily picked up on.

"Your license and your registration, ma'am?" He reached his hand through the window, palm up toward her.

"What did I do?"

"We'll start with speeding," he said.

He thought she muttered, "Great," but he couldn't be sure because she was leaning across the console to reach the glove compartment. Her hair flipped at his hand and he pulled back slightly, catching a hint of some flowery scent. He watched her hit the release button and this time he knew she said, "Well, damn it," before sitting back and grabbing a purse she'd set on the passenger seat. She tore through the worn leather satchel, pulled out a wallet, then produced a driver's license. "There you go," she said, handing it to him through the window.

"The registration?"

"I can't find it," she said, stuffing things back into her purse.

"Keep looking," he countered, then left to go back to the squad car. He opened the door, but stayed outside and reached in for the handset. Before he could put in the call, the radio was talking to him. He flipped a button and fell into the pattern of law enforcement in Silver Creek. No fancy codes, no "Roger" this or "Roger" that. "What's going on?"

"Got your information," Wes said. "Guess what? You got a hot BMW there. It's on the sheet out of Chicago. Stolen eight days ago from one Barton Wise."

Joshua knew criminals came in all shapes and sizes. Even with deep blue eyes. "Are you sure the numbers match?" he asked.

"Oh, they match. Checked them twice."

"Okay," Joshua said, raising the license the woman had given him. "Get whatever you can on one Riley Jane Shaw. She's out of Chicago, twenty-six."

"She?"

"Yeah, she, and she's alone in the car. I'll bring her in, but send Rollie out with his tow truck, one mile north of the far corner of Jack's place."

"Do you want backup?" Wes asked seriously.

He would have said, "Forget it," but he'd seen it happen too often—a cop making a routine traffic stop, then being shot for his lack of caution. "Sure, come on out," he said. "I'll wait for you."

"You got it."

Joshua put the handset back, then stood by the squad car, reading and rereading the license in his hand. Auburn hair, blue eyes, five feet six inches tall. He stared at her picture, at a younger version of how she looked now, with dark, fairly short hair softly feathered around her face. No anger there, no impatience. Pretty. He glanced at the BMW and could see her watching him in the rearview mirror. Pretty, and driving a stolen car.

He didn't make a move toward the BMW until he saw the other cruiser coming down the road toward them. He noticed the woman in the car shift, looking ahead of her, watching the cruiser cut across the road and come to a stop inches from her bumper, nose to nose. She twisted around to look back at him. The heavy window tinting hid any facial expressions, but her body language screamed nervousness.

He motioned to Wes to stop as he got out of the car, and stay where he was, with the cruiser door between him and the suspect. He pushed Riley Shaw's license into the pocket of his jacket, then unsnapped his holster lock and headed back to the BMW. The window was gliding down as he looked in and met those deep blue eyes.

"What's going on?" she asked.

Joshua didn't miss the fact that her right hand was on the steering wheel and her left hand was out of sight.

"Hands in sight," he said.

She quickly raised both her hands, palms toward him. "Hey, just a minute. I—"

"Please step out of the car," he said, his right hand hovering by his holstered gun. He saw her eyes dart to the gun, then back to his face. Now she was scared and that could bring any action, from trying to run, striking out at him or collapsing into tears. He didn't want any of that to happen. He just wanted her out of the car with her hands empty.

"Why?" she asked, not moving, her hands still in the air.

He reached for the door handle and pulled, but it was locked. "Please unlock the door, ma'am."

"Sure, sure," she said, hitting the automatic lock opener and it clicked.

He pulled the door open and stood back as far as he could from the woman. She squinted up at him, then stepped out into the frigid air. Her shirt looked as though it was made of thin cotton and her well-worn Levi's showed a strategic rip at one knee. Somehow he thought the rip was accidental and not an intentional statement of fashion. She was wearing running shoes, no socks and even though her license had said she was twenty-six, she looked like a teenager.

"Step clear of the car, ma'am," Joshua said as he let go of the door and moved back, motioning to her left.

She darted a look at the other squad car, then back at him. "Please, tell me what's going on," she said as she took a step toward him.

"Turn around and face the car. Place your hands on the top, palms down. This car was reported stolen from Chicago, and unless you're Mrs. Barton Wise, you're under arrest for suspicion of grand theft auto."

"This is crazy!" she gasped. "I'm just driving this car for delivery to San Diego. I came around the long way. I got lost, then realized I had to cut back this way to get on the route to Las Vegas." She spoke quickly in a breathless voice. "I'm just delivering it. It's not stolen."

He was willing to listen, if she could prove it. It would make his life simpler at the moment. "Okay, show me the paperwork."

She frowned at him. "Paperwork?"

"The agreement you signed, the bond you put up, anything to prove that you have the right to be in this car."

She swallowed hard. "Okay, sure, but I need to get it," she said, holding her hands up, palms toward him. "I just need to get my bag."

"Okay, slowly," he said with a nod.

He watched her carefully as she reached inside the back of the car and pulled out a duffel bag. She held it up to him. "It's in here," she said.

"Okay, get it."

She unzipped the bag, dug into it, and he found himself holding his breath until she pulled out an envelope. She opened it and held it out so he could see the contents. Inside, there was a stack of bills and a piece of paper.

"Take out the paper and put down the bag."

She shivered as the wind gusted, but she did as she was told, pulling out the piece of paper, then dropping the duffel at her feet on the icy shoulder of the road. She held the paper out to him. "Here. This is all I have."

He took it, glanced at Wes, then shook the paper to open it. It was mostly blank, but at the top was a San Diego phone number, the name Mindy Sullivan and a date, eight days from today. It looked as if it had been printed off of a computer. "What does this prove?"

"That's the number I'm supposed to call when I get to San Diego. They'll tell me where to take the car."

"And the money in the envelope?"

"It's the payment for my services, combined with my money that…that I put in with it."

He didn't realize until then how much he wanted her story to be true. But she hadn't shown him anything that would prove it. "Sorry, that doesn't mean anything."

"It means I answered an ad in the paper to drive this car from Chicago to San Diego, and I'm doing that. Call Mindy Sullivan and ask her. Her attorney in Chicago hired me." She looked relieved. "That's it, the attorney. Call him. He'll tell you this is all a big mistake."

Wes was coming toward them now. "Everything okay?" he asked.

Joshua said "Fine" at the same time the woman said "No, it's not."

He ignored her statement and asked Wes, "Was there a Mindy Sullivan on the sheet for the BMW?"

"No, boss, the only name was Barton Wise."

He looked back at Riley Shaw and realized she was close to tears. He didn't want to deal with a hysterical female, even if she was a car thief. "You can't do this," she muttered.

He hesitated, something a cop should never do. "If you have anything to prove you didn't steal this car, give it to me now. Otherwise I have no option but take you in."

"The attorney in Chicago," she said. "Just call him. You can check with him and find out this is a mistake."

"I can't do that from here, so we'll go to the station," he said. "Now, turn around and place both hands on the car."

"Please, this is insane. I didn't steal this car."

He moved closer. "We can do this the easy way or the hard way. It's up to you," he said as he looked down into her face. He could see she was shaking. Fear? She could just be cold. Her clothes were little protection against the gusting wind. "Let's do this the easy way."

RILEY CLOSED her eyes for a long moment to try to calm herself and shut out the sight of the man right in front of her. His clothing was heavy, but even so she could tell he was a lean man, maybe six feet tall, with roughly angled features. He was wearing reflective sunglasses, so she had no idea what his eyes were like, and a uniform cap covered most of his hair. All in all, there was no hint of softness in the man.

The hard way or the easy way? Maybe he didn't care which way this played out. But she did. It was a mistake. A crazy mistake. A misstep on her way to San Diego. She'd call the attorney and wipe that smug look of control off the cop's face. She looked at her own reflection in his glasses and thought she looked like a vagrant. She hadn't dressed to impress for the trip.

"What about my money?" she asked, holding up the envelope. "It's mine."

"I'll take it," he said, and did. He put the paper back in the envelope, then shoved it into the pocket of his green uniform jacket. "I'll give you a receipt at the station."

"You bet you will," she muttered.

"Miss Shaw, I'll personally make sure you get

every cent if your story checks out and we release you," he said. "Now, turn around, hands on the car."

Riley uttered a single word that she never used, then turned to slap both of her hands palms down on the cold top of the black car. She'd come so far, but at this moment, she felt as if she'd slipped back into a past she'd tried to bury for ten years.

She was startled when he touched her from behind, his hands on her shoulders, skimming over her, light but thorough. Down both of her arms, down her sides, to her waist, to her hips, then down and on both sides of her legs. She closed her eyes tightly, enduring the touch, praying for it to end.

Once the frisking was over, though, he snapped a handcuff on her wrist, then pulled her other hand down and back to secure it. "Okay, let's go," he said so close she felt the air vibrate with his words.

She turned slowly, taking time to focus, to build the anger that smoldered in her. There was no way she was going to dissolve into tears in front of a cop. "What's your name?" she asked.

"Joshua Pierce."

"Badge number?"

"The name's enough," he murmured.

"Okay, but you're going to regret this."

He shook his head. "Adding 'threatening a police officer in the commission of his duties' is not going to help anything."

She shrugged, tugging at the handcuffs. "I think it's illegal to let a prisoner freeze to death," she muttered.

"We don't want that to happen." He caught her by her upper arm and led her to his squad car. Opening the back door, he put his hand on the top of her head to ease her down and in, then waited for her to scoot over on the hard seat. She shifted, settled and stared straight ahead.

He opened his door, then called to the other cop. "Wait for Rollie to get here, then come back to the station."

"Are you cool with this?" he asked, motioning to her in the car.

This obviously wasn't big city if a cop used the word *cool*.

"Very cool," he said to the other man, then slipped in behind the wheel.

Riley felt him study her in the rearview mirror, through the wire mesh separation in the cruiser. "What about my things?" she asked.

"They'll be secured," he said, then asked, "Are you comfortable?"

She looked at him, those reflective glasses driving her crazy. She hated not being able to see his eyes. "Cool," she muttered.

She thought she saw the hint of a smile shadow his lips for a moment before he pulled out around the BMW. He waved to the other officer, then headed south. He shifted and she knew he was looking at her in the mirror again.

"Nice clean car," she said.

That smile was almost there again. "Thanks."

She looked around the interior. "Dated, but dead-on clean."

"Are you a connoisseur of police cruisers?"

She'd seen a few in her life, but this was not the first

time she'd been in one and she wasn't guilty of anything. She'd done everything to never ride in a cop car again, but here she was. The last time, she'd been guilty as heck, but not this time. The last time she'd gotten into the stolen car knowing it was stolen, and gone for a joyride with three kids she'd known she shouldn't trust. The last time she'd been arrested, she'd thought she'd be in jail for the rest of her life. And she might have been, if she hadn't been rescued.

Riley looked at the cop who said his name was Joshua Pierce, and knew that there wouldn't be a rescue this time. He took off his uniform cap, tossed it on the front seat, exposing thick dark hair flecked with gray at the temples, and she finally looked away and out the side window. A stone fence ran along the road then stopped at an elaborate entrance to some sort of estate or resort. They even had a guard by massive wooden gates. The guard looked up, waved, then glanced in the back seat at her. His hand stilled in the air.

"You don't get too many criminals around here, do you?" she asked.

"Not usually," he murmured.

"I bet you'll get some sort of medal for arresting a hardened criminal ready to take over this town."

He looked at her in the rearview mirror and she saw her own image reflected in his glasses. "One can only hope so," he murmured.

"That's a joke, Officer, like this whole thing is a joke," she muttered. One thing she'd learned as a teenager living on the streets was to keep things like fear to yourself. Never show weakness. And when she'd rebuilt her life, the same thing applied. When she'd had her interviews at the college with prospective employers once she'd earned her degree in physical therapy, she'd made very sure she didn't let them know how scared she was or how desperate she was for a good job.

"This isn't a joke, Miss Shaw," he said.

She shrugged, but caught her handcuffs on the hard plastic of the seat. She looked out at the scenery, the rock fence gone as they slipped into what looked like a typical skiing community with shops and houses, ski lifts that were crowded with skiers, and more shops and restaurants. Everything looked determinedly "cute" and postcard-perfect.

Finally they arrived at a security fence that swung open as they approached. The squad car pulled in next to the other cars in the lot and the cop exited and came around to where she sat.

He pulled open her door and the cold air cut into the car. She shivered as she ducked to get out, her movements awkward without the use of her hands. He steadied her by holding her upper arm, and once she was on her feet they headed for the building.

Within a minute they were inside and she was grateful for the warmth. She looked around at the wide central room that held several desks, lines of filing cabinets, and fronted what was probably the entry to the jail. A long, dark-wood reception desk separated the entry from the main room. This jail was anything but cute, like the town. It had worn wooden floors, wainscotting done in what looked like fake cherrywood, off-white walls adorned with Wanted posters and a huge message board.

All police stations had that dull look to them, as if hope died in them. But she wasn't going to let that happen to her. She'd prove her innocence and be back on the road in no time.

Chapter Two

The place looked empty until Joshua let Riley go and she heard, "Hey, there." She turned to see a cop coming out of a rear area, through a metal lockdown door. The cell area. She knew without asking. He left the heavy door open and headed across to them, speaking to Joshua as he got closer. "Wes said you'd be back," he said. He was older, maybe in his mid-fifties or so, with a discernable paunch under his uniform and a lopsided way of walking.

"Charlie, this is Riley Shaw. Miss Shaw, this is Deputy Sloan, Acting Sheriff around here."

Riley nodded to the man, but he spoke directly to Joshua. "Is this the GTA you called in?"

"Yes, I picked her up just past the inn, driving a stolen BMW."

He shook his head and laughed gruffly. "Well, I'll be. You never know, do you? Do you want to take care of the case?"

"It's not a case," Riley said quickly. "I'm not staying."

Charlie looked at her and actually smiled again.

"Well, miss, I think you will be, even if it's just while we straighten out this grand theft auto business." He came around to undo her handcuffs, then tugged the metal bracelets off of her. "We'll get these off, then get you settled in a cell until we can sort this out."

"No," she said quickly, pulling her freed hands to the front and rubbing at her wrists. "No." She was ready to dig in and make them drag her to the lockdown area.

Joshua exhaled. "The cell is temporary, just until we see if you're going to be booked or not."

"No, please, just…" She looked around, the idea of being locked up making her physically sick to her stomach. "Can't I just sit in a chair? I mean, you can handcuff me to the chair or the desk. You know, one of those bars you screw to a desk? Anything. Just put the handcuffs back on and—" She held her hands out to Joshua, wrists together. "Just secure me anywhere out here."

"Sorry, you'll have to go by our rules while you're here," he said, and slipped off his sunglasses.

Damn, she'd wanted to see his eyes before, but when she met his unprotected gaze, eyes that were green with hazel flecks, she tensed horribly. Her stomach clenched so sharply that she had to press a hand to her middle. "Oh, man, I'm going to be sick," she said in a low voice.

"Don't start histrionics," Joshua said as he tucked the sunglasses into his jacket pocket, then looked at Charlie. "Is a cell ready?"

"No, I mean it," she gasped, swallowing hard to keep the nausea at bay. She was going to be sick, right here and now. "I'm sick. I…"

She was looking at Joshua, the sickness coming in waves. Suddenly the world began to spin and blur, and before she could figure out what was going on, she was falling forward. She hit something solid, then she was being held and supported, but that didn't stop her descent into a black void.

JOSHUA HAD BARELY put his sunglasses away when he saw Riley Shaw go horribly pale, then proceed to faint dead away in his arms. At first he thought it was a ploy of some sort, but the instant she was in his arms, he knew it was for real. He gathered her deadweight, shifted to lift her in his arms and spoke to Charlie. "Get the door to the cell open."

"What's going on?" Charlie asked as he rushed ahead of Joshua into the lockdown area.

"She fainted," he said, following Charlie.

"Which cell?" Charlie asked.

Joshua looked down the aisle with its row of six cells. Most were seldom used, and they were cookie-cutter copies of each other, with cots, toilets, sinks and one table each. He opted for the closest one. "Cell One," he said, and Charlie flipped the switch on the wall to release the lock. He pulled the barred entry open and let Joshua into the eight-by-ten-foot cell.

He carried her to the stripped cot along the back wall and eased her down onto the bare mattress. She fell limply onto the cot and he hunkered down to press the tips of his fingers to the side of her throat. She looked painfully pale, but her pulse was there, light but steady.

"I'll call the clinic and ask Doc to come over and check her out," Charlie said, and hurried back into the main room.

When Joshua touched Riley on her cool cheek, she stirred slightly and he eased back. Dark lashes arched on her pale skin, then they fluttered and her eyes opened. They were unfocused at first, but at the same time they started to sharpen, she jerked up, almost hitting Joshua in the process. He reached for her shoulders and tried to ease her back down. "Hey, take it easy," he said.

She was shaking, but refused to lie down. Her eyes darted around the cell. "Oh, no," she breathed, and twisted to face him as she swiped at his hands. "What happened?"

He pulled back, but stayed hunkered down and at eye level with her. "You fainted. Just take it easy. The doctor's coming."

"No, no doctor. I don't need a doctor." She shook her head. "I just need to not be here."

He knew the feeling, but that didn't change facts. "Charlie wants the doctor to check you out."

She released a breath on a shuddering hiss. "I'm okay," she said, and twisted, pushing with her hands to get to her feet.

He moved back as she stood, but he didn't miss the unsteadiness in her stance. "I told you to—"

Charlie was back at the door to the lockdown area. "Doc's on his way. Says to keep an eye on her, not to leave her alone." The buzzer from dispatch sounded on the speaker. "Stay here with her," Charlie said briskly over his shoulder as he took off on a jog to take the call in dispatch.

Joshua turned to Riley. She was very still, her arms clutched around her chest, and she was looking right at him with startling blue eyes. "Lie down. The doctor will be here soon," he said, automatically reaching to help her sit.

Before he could make contact, she swiped at his hand, striking him on the wrist. "Don't. You can't do this," she said.

"Miss Shaw, I'm not doing this because I'm enjoying it." He rubbed at his wrist and stopped himself before he said, "I'm just doing my duty." He remembered hating his dad saying that when he was growing up. "I'm just trying to make this as easy for all of us as I can."

She bit her lip and slowly sank onto the cot, but she stayed sitting up and stared at the floor. "Listen, I didn't steal that car. I really didn't."

"Okay. I'll make inquiries, and if that's true, I'll apologize to you and fill your gas tank on the way out of town."

Her eyes lifted and he met her blue gaze. Why in the hell did he feel like such a heel for only doing what he'd said he'd do?

"Well, polish up on your apology and find some cheap gas," she murmured.

The vulnerability he'd seen in her when she'd fainted and after she'd come around was gone. It was replaced by a hard look and sarcasm. "We'll see," was all he trusted himself to say.

Charlie was back. "Got problems at the lifts. Kids getting out of hand. Rollie got the car and Wes is on his way to the lifts. You stay and cover the calls, and take care of Doc when he gets here." Charlie glanced at Riley, then, with a nod to her, left.

Joshua looked back at Riley. "While we wait for Doc to get here, I'll make some phone calls to see what I can find out."

He moved toward the cell door, but as he turned back to say one more thing to her, he stopped. She was right behind him, reminding him of a puppy dog who wouldn't stay put and insisted on being at your heels. "Don't leave me here," she said, that vulnerability there for a flashing instant in her blue eyes.

"Miss Shaw, you can't—"

She lifted her chin with determination. "But the doctor said not to leave me alone."

He'd forgotten all about that. "You'll be fine."

"No, I could faint again." She pointed at the cement floor. "If I hit that instead of having you to catch me…" She met his gaze without blinking. "I could really get hurt, and if I get hurt because you're negligent and you've brought me in here wrongly, well…" She let her words trail off with the threat implied instead of stated.

Vulnerable? Not hardly. "Okay, you can come out with me until a deputy gets back or the doctor arrives."

Without a word, she went around him, and he found himself in the ludicrous position of following the prisoner out of the lockdown area into the main squad room. She hesitated, then turned to look at him. "Where do you want to chain me?" she asked with what seemed to be complete seriousness.

He walked around her and crossed to his dad's office near the side entry hall. "In here," he said, letting her pass him into the work space. As he went in after her, he shrugged out of his jacket and hung it on a hook by the door, then turned.

This had been his dad's office for as long as he could remember. It had seemed dark and threatening to him when he'd been a kid, but now it looked tired and mellow. There were worn leather chairs, a wooden desk scarred from thirty years of wear, and filing cabinets that he hadn't even looked in since filling in at the station. The bottom half of the wall that it shared with the main room was dark wood; the upper part was glass, lined with plain old horizontal blinds. His dad had always kept them open. They were still open.

"You can sit there," he said, motioning to one of two straight-backed wooden chairs that faced the desk.

She took a seat, then looked up at him and said, "Go ahead. Do your duty."

She was serious, but he couldn't be. He found himself smiling at her. "Please, just sit there and be still." He moved around the desk to drop into the leather swivel chair, and turned to Riley.

"No chains or handcuffs?" she asked.

"No whips and torture, either, if you'll just promise me you'll stay put until the doctor gets here."

"I will, if you promise me you'll call Chicago and find out the truth."

He was more than ready to do that. He reached for a notepad and pen. "Okay. First, why don't you give me the name and number of the attorney who supposedly hired you to drive the car?"

She frowned intently as she sat forward on the wooden seat and pressed the palms of her hands against the edge of his desk. "It begins with an N. Nilland. No." She closed her eyes tightly and whispered, "Think, think, think." Then she said, "Nyland." Her eyes opened. "Alvin Nyland."

He had his pen ready. "What's his number?"

She shrugged and he could see her fingers pressing hard against the wooden top of the desk. "I don't know. I didn't think to bring it. But surely he'd be listed. He's got a huge office in Chicago, takes up a lot of floors in this towering building by the lake, and there are four or five partners in the firm's name. You know, one of those big, overblown, fancy, money-making law firms?"

Yes, he knew very well what she meant. "Okay, what are the names in the big, overblown, fancy, money-making law firm?"

"I don't remember, but it sure sounded important and his name's part of it. Not at the top, but second or third, I think." She let go of the desk and motioned to the phone. "Just call and give his name to Information. They should have a listing for him. Alvin Nyland," she repeated, and slowly spelled out the last name letter by letter.

He lifted the receiver and put in a call to Information for Chicago and asked for Alvin Nyland, Attorney. They came up with the number right away, and he hit the button to dial it through, then heard a voice on the other end. "Good afternoon. Wallace, Levin, Geisler, Nyland and Yen. How may I direct your call?"

"Alvin Nyland, please."

There was a click, soft music, then another voice picked up. "Mr. Nyland's office."

"Mr. Nyland, please."

"I'm sorry, Mr. Nyland isn't available. May I take a message?"

He knew well enough that not being available could mean anything from being in the restroom to being dead. "I need to speak with him. It's important."

Riley was sitting forward now, her elbows on the desk, and he didn't miss the way she crossed her fingers, much the way an earnest child would. "Is he there?" she asked in a tense whisper.

He shook his head as the woman on the other end of the line said, "I'm sorry, sir, he's out of the office."

"Where is he?" he asked.

"May I ask who's calling?"

"Deputy Joshua Pierce from the Silver Creek Police Department in Silver Creek, Nevada. I need to speak to Mr. Nyland about an important matter."

"Well, I'm so sorry, that's not possible. He's on vacation and out of touch."

"Where?"

She hesitated, then said, "Florida."

Joshua exhaled. "Okay, maybe you can help me."

"Any way I can," she said quickly.

"I need to have some verification about an arrangement he made for a car delivery."

"A car delivery?" she asked.

"To San Diego. A new BMW sedan." He watched Riley as he explained the situation. "I need his verification that Miss Shaw is supposed to have it in her possession, and an explanation about the car being reported stolen."

"Sir, I don't know what you're talking about. Mr. Nyland is an investment attorney, and he certainly wouldn't be involved in car transfers."

"Do you know the name Riley Shaw?"

"No, sir. I don't."

"When will Mr. Nyland be back?"

"I don't know, sir. I'm sorry. He just said next week sometime."

Before Joshua hung up, he asked, "Does he have clients named Mindy Sullivan or Barton Wise?"

"Sir, I can't tell you about his clients. That's privileged information."

"All I need is a yes or no, nothing else. If I have to, I'll get the Chicago police up to your office with the proper legal papers. If you'll just tell me yes or no, we'll drop it."

"Well, just a minute," she said, and the music came back on the line.

Riley was nibbling nervously on her bottom lip and he had the idea while the secretary was searching her database, that Riley Shaw was either a great liar or a true innocent. As a cop, he prided himself on being able to read people, but this woman was hard to peg.

"Deputy?" the receptionist asked, interrupting Joshua's thoughts.

"Yes, I'm here."

"All I can say is, I have never personally heard of Mindy Sullivan or Barton Wise."

"I appreciate that," he said, then gave her his number. "If Mr. Nyland calls in for anything, could you ask him to contact me immediately?"

"Yes, sir, of course," she said.

He thanked her and hung up, all the while watching Riley sink back in her chair. "Nothing," he said, and she glared at him as if he'd failed in the most miserable way possible. He explained, "He's on vacation in Florida and out of touch, and his receptionist doesn't remember Sullivan or Wise."

Riley felt as if she had fallen into some black hole. "I swear, he's the one who gave me the money and the directions and said to take the car to San Diego."

"Where in San Diego?"

"I'm supposed to call Mindy Sullivan when I get to the city, and she'll tell me where to deliver it." Her stomach was hurting again and she wrapped her arms around it. "I can't believe this," she breathed, rocking front to back slowly.

He looked worried again and she knew she must look horrible. "Miss Shaw—"

"Riley. My name's Riley."

Before she could tell him to call Mindy Sullivan, a buzzer sounded and Joshua was up and heading out of his office. "Hey, Gordie," he said. "We're in here."

Riley stared at the worn wooden top of the desk until she heard another voice right behind her. "Okay, so what's going on?" a man's deep voice asked.

She twisted around to see a tall man bundled up in a suede jacket with a heavy fur collar, a matching fur hat pulled low on his head. He was gripping a stereotypical black bag in one hand; with the other, he skimmed off his fur hat. He was pleasant-looking, maybe in his late thirties, with irregular features and an aura of kindness. Riley hardly ever thought that about anyone she met.

"Gordie, the prisoner fainted," Joshua said, coming to the other side of Riley's chair.

The doctor had sharp blue eyes and an easy smile as he studied her. "I'm Dr. Gordon." He flicked a glance at Joshua. "Although some persist in calling me Gordie." He crouched so that he and Riley were eye-to-eye. "So tell me what happened."

"I don't know. I just fainted. I've never fainted before," she said. "I've never even come close."

"No. I mean, why did they arrest you?"

She blinked at him, wondering if he was joking. But he seemed serious as he took some things out of his bag and started examining her while she answered. "They say I stole a car."

He reached for her wrist, pressed his fingertips to her pulse and studied a watch on his other wrist. "So you're a car thief, huh?"

"No, I'm not."

He chuckled and glanced at Joshua. "They're all innocent, aren't they?"

She looked up at her arresting officer, who was watching the two of them. She could take the doctor joking, but she couldn't take the smile on Joshua's face. "This isn't a joke," she muttered.

Joshua sobered, but it was the doctor who spoke up. "Well, if you take life too seriously, you're doomed."

She stared at him. "I just want to know why I fainted."

As he got out a stethoscope, he explained, "I don't have a clue yet. Headache?"

"No."

"Nauseous?"

"A bit."

"You're not diabetic?"

"No."

"Pregnant?"

She could feel the fire in her cheeks. "No."

He pressed the cool stethoscope to her chest where her shirt was open. "Drugs?"

"No," she muttered tightly. "Never."

"Okay, when's the last time you ate?" he asked, frowning as he listened to her heart.

"A few hours ago, maybe three or four."

"What did you eat?"

She shrugged. "I don't remember. Oh, a corn dog, some nachos, a soda and some candy bars."

"You're lucky to be breathing after eating that," he murmured as he put the stethoscope back in his bag.

"It was either that or sausage on a stick and jelly beans."

He smiled. "The lesser of two evils?" He took out a blood pressure cuff, tugged up her sleeve, then fastened the cuff on her upper arm.

"Definitely," she said.

"Just relax," he said as he pumped up the cuff. "Think of sunny beaches and lazy days under a palm tree." He slowly deflated the cuff, listened, then finally undid it. "Good blood pressure."

With all the stress she'd had since the squad car flicked on its flashing lights and siren, she figured having a normal blood pressure was a near miracle. He took her temperature with a digital thermometer, then placed it back in his bag with the other equipment.

"What's wrong with me?" she asked.

He stood and looked down at her. "Besides a horrendous diet, my guess is you fainted."

"Well, that's a no-brainer," she muttered.

"Sorry," he said with a smile. "I've been taking care of too many skiers who forget to get out of the way of a tree, then expect me to say they were tricked by the damn tree. It couldn't be they're terrible skiers." He shrugged. "Honestly, I can't find a thing wrong with you, except your diet. What was happening when you fainted?"

She nodded toward Joshua as she tugged her sleeve down. "*He* was going to put me in a cell."

The doctor considered her words, then looked at Joshua. "You were locking her up?"

"She was driving a stolen car."

"I was not," she said quickly. "It's not stolen."

The doctor looked back at Riley. "Ah, therein lies the rub."

A doctor who quoted Shakespeare? "Rub or no rub, I didn't steal it," she said tightly. "And he'd know that if he ever got around to doing his job and finished checking things out." She exhaled. "I think it's a violation of my rights to hold me and do next to nothing to find out the truth. Someone needs to teach him how to play cop."

"He's not playing, and he's not just a cop. Back in his real life, he is…well, was, the head crime-buster in Atlanta." He snapped his bag closed and picked it up. "Big office, maybe a big career in politics. Big man."

She looked at Joshua. "Atlanta?" He just nodded. "How did you end up here?" she asked.

"All roads lead to Silver Creek," the doctor said.

Hers sure had. "Too bad," she murmured.

"Oh, Silver Creek's a nice place, Miss Shaw," the doctor said. "And my theory is, if you're born here, you end up here. It's that simple."

She looked at Joshua again, but he spoke to Gordie. "That's enough, Gordie. Thanks for coming."

"Just make sure she eats something decent, something bland, and have her checked on periodically." He looked at her with a shake of his head. "Sure hate to see a pretty thing like you in a dump like this."

"Me, too," she said.

He pulled his hat back on, reached for his bag, then spoke to Joshua. "I'm on my way to set another leg." With that, he left.

Riley wished she could follow him, head out the door, close it behind her and keep going, all the way to San Diego. But she was left behind sitting at a desk, trying to figure a way out of the nightmare that had become her life in the past hour or so.

Joshua stood over her and she finally realized he was staring at her. "What?"

"I was going to ask how you're feeling," he said as he went around the desk to take his seat again.

"I'd feel better if you were as efficient as the doctor."

That brought out a bark of laughter. "Gordie? Oh, he talks a good game. He always has."

"At least he can see how stupid this all is," she muttered, then added, "Now, are you going to contact

Chicago Police or not? They can get this all cleared up."

"Chicago," he said as he reached for a thick book on the desk, flipped it open, then reached for the phone. He punched in a number and introduced himself to whoever picked up on the other end. Reading off the information about the car, Joshua ended with, "I need to speak with whoever's in charge of the investigation." He listened for a moment, then said, "Sure, put me through."

While Joshua spoke and took notes, Riley sat there wishing this was all just a dream. But once he'd hung up and addressed her again, Riley knew this was a nightmare come to life.

She was beginning to feel horribly sick again, and couldn't think straight. She just lunged for the phone, and the next thing she knew, she had grabbed his hand so tightly hers was aching.

Chapter Three

Joshua was startled by Riley's actions, and his hand froze, her hand over his, holding on to it so tightly it was almost painful. Their eyes met, and he saw her shock at her own actions in the deep blue. Slowly, she let go of him, sinking back and down into the chair.

He let go of the phone and said, "The car's been stolen. Detective Gagne will contact the owner for verification."

"When?"

"As soon as he can and he'll call back when he does."

"Meanwhile?"

"I'm to hold you here."

What little color she had left drained from her face and for a moment he thought she was going to faint again. But she took a shaky breath, then said, "Okay, I understand how this looks. I really do. But you're making a huge mistake."

He tented his fingers to look at her over them. A novice criminal? A first-time job? A truly bad car thief? An innocent woman? He wished he knew. "Is there anyone who can back up your story? Your employer? Family? Friends? Someone who knew all about this?"

She stared at him, then finally shook her head. "No. My employer is still my future employer and I'll lose the job before I even get it if a cop calls about me stealing a car. I don't have any family, and I didn't really tell anyone about this car-delivery thing."

"Alvin Nyland isn't available," he said, trying to figure out how a person like Riley Shaw ended up totally alone in this world.

"If he is *my* Alvin Nyland," she murmured.

"What does that mean?"

She shrugged. "I've been thinking. What if he's a fraud? He didn't give me any papers. He checked on me, and I didn't check on him. We met in the evening at his office, and no one else was there. He gave me the paper and directions." Her color seemed almost normal now, but he didn't like the way she hugged her arms around her middle and hunched forward. When she spoke again, she was almost speaking to herself. "What if it's all a lie, a setup? What if I got roped into being part of some car-theft ring? What if they get people like me to drive stolen cars to a destination, and if they get there, fine, and if not, the criminals would never be involved?" She looked up at him. "That happens, doesn't it?"

Joshua couldn't figure out why he had the impulse to make things better for her, or why, when he heard her take a shuddering breath, he hated what he was doing. "It could," he conceded as he pushed the phone toward her. "You still have your one call."

She stared at the phone as if she didn't know what

to do with it, then suddenly reached for it. "Where's that paper I gave you with Mindy Sullivan's phone number on it?" she asked.

He retrieved it from his jacket and handed it to her.

Watching as Riley made the call, Joshua noticed her face tug into a frown as she hit the disconnect button. Very carefully, she redialed the number and listened. She put the receiver back in the cradle so hard that plastic cracked against plastic and she hugged her arms around her middle again.

"No answer?" he asked.

She shook her head. "The…the number isn't working," she whispered.

Before he could respond, Riley stood and faced him. "I think I'm going to be sick," she mumbled, then put a hand over her mouth.

"Are you serious?"

She nodded without saying anything and Joshua wasn't taking any chances this time. He had her by the arm, leading her out of the office and to the women's restroom. Riley pulled free of him and hurried ahead, but instead of going into a stall, she went to the nearest sink and grabbed the sides of the white enamel, her head forward, swallowing hard.

"If you're going to be sick, use—"

"I'm okay," she whispered. She splashed cold water on her face, dampening the loose tendrils of hair that had escaped her ponytail and dripping down on to her shirt, darkening the cotton. She took several deep breaths, then reached for paper towels from the dispenser on the wall and pressed them to her face.

If it hadn't been bad enough to have had a woman

faint dead away in his arms, now the same woman was close to being sick. He could see each breath she took, the way she shuddered on a final sigh as she pulled the towels down and crushed them into a ball in her hand.

"Are you okay?" he asked, feeling ridiculous standing there.

"I'm sorry," she mumbled as she dropped the towels in the wastebasket, then held her hands under the cold water, just letting it wash over her skin.

He saw her reflection in the distorted mirror over the sink. Bright color dotted both cheeks and dark smudges shadowed her eyes. She finally turned off the water, dried her hands on more towels, tossed those towels away and turned to him. He didn't miss how she still held to the sink with her right hand.

"Do you need me to call Gordie?" he asked.

"No, he can't help me." She turned back to her reflection in the mirror and brushed at her hair. He didn't miss the unsteadiness in her hand. Damn it, he didn't want to feel protective, but he did. She met his gaze in the mottled mirror. "Do you usually escort female prisoners into the bathroom?"

That errant feeling of protectiveness fled, replaced by annoyance. "The only reason I brought you in here was that the cells were farther away and I thought—" He cut off his own words, impatient with himself for feeling the need to explain his actions to her. "Next time, I'll take you to your cell. There's a toilet and sink there."

The color in her cheeks deepened. "Oh, joy. All the comforts of home," she muttered.

It was a good thing he was only doing this job as a

fill-in for his dad. He'd been a cop most of his adult life, but didn't want to be doing it now, and especially not with her. "You know, it might be better if you just told me what's going on, and maybe we can work something out."

"Are you offering me a deal?" she asked, continuing to grip the edge of the sink. She turned to him.

"The acting sheriff would have to do that. But, if you tell me the truth, maybe I can talk to the higher-ups and work something out for you."

"I bare my soul and you give me a break?" She regarded him without blinking. "Your acting sheriff will cut me a deal?"

"If you tell me everything, we can go from there."

She exhaled harshly, with obvious exasperation. "I've told you everything, so where do we go from here?"

He shrugged. "I hold you until Chicago gets back to me on what they want done."

"When will they get back to you?"

"No idea."

"Meanwhile, you just hold me here? What about booking me and my arraignment? Isn't it a fact you have seventy-two hours to arraign me after booking? There isn't an open-ended time limit, is there?"

Damn it, she wasn't a novice at this. She knew her stuff. "If I book you now, yeah, it's seventy-two hours."

"What do you mean, *if* you book me now?"

"I can book you, get it going, then it's on the record. And we'll have to arraign you on the evidence we have now."

"Do I hear an 'or' in that statement?"

He wasn't at all sure he could make this work, but he threw out a tentative deal that he knew would be a hard sell to Charlie. His dad would have gone for it, hands down, but Charlie was tougher, a more letter-of-the-law type cop. But he was also reasonable. "If I can talk the acting sheriff into it, maybe we can hold off on the booking, just detain you for a day or so, and if it comes up that you're telling the truth, then this never happened. If we book you, and in two days we find out you're telling the truth, then we've got a bit of a mess on our hands. It'll show you were picked up and booked and—"

"A day or two?" she asked.

"Chicago should have something by tomorrow, the next day at the latest. Then we can do what's necessary."

She was silent for a long moment, staring at the floor, then she met his gaze. "None of this will go on my record if what I've told you is the truth?"

He dug himself further into the offer. "None of it."

"And the acting sheriff will agree?"

He shrugged. "I'll talk to him, lay it out for him, but it will have to be his decision."

"But you think he'll agree?"

"There's a good chance he will."

She stood straighter. "Okay, I'll wait. I'll let you detain me until Chicago straightens this out."

Joshua didn't know if he was relieved or being a real fool. He just hoped Charlie would go for the delayed booking. "Okay, let's get you settled."

"Can I wait in your office until you find out if he'll wait on the booking?" she asked.

"First of all, it's not my office, I'm just using it for

now, and second, I don't know when I can run it past Charlie, and since you're being detained, that means you're being held, and that means, you're being held in a cell."

He saw that urge in her to argue, to fight him, but she finally said, "Let's get this over with," and went around him to the door. Once again he was the one following as she walked out into the squad room. From behind, he noticed her slender hips in the faded denim, the movement of her body as she walked determinedly toward the lockdown security door as if going there had been her decision all along.

He heard someone talking near the front entrance, but didn't take his eyes off Riley. They went into the cell area and she stopped abruptly. Quick sidestepping kept him from running into her back. "Which cell?" she asked.

He motioned to the one he'd carried her into earlier. The door was still open. "That one's fine." He could see her hesitate, then take a deep breath, as if preparing to plunge into deep water, then she went inside. She turned just inside the door and he didn't go in after her.

He looked at her, framed by the metal frame and the bars on either side. He'd seen enough prisoners walk into a cell, and he thought he was immune to any response beyond the required caution with any alleged criminal. But as he looked at Riley Shaw, he realized the picture didn't add up. Something was amiss, but he wasn't about to stand here and figure it out. He'd let Charlie deal with her. "How about some food?"

She looked from side to side, then went to the cot

on the back wall, sat on the edge and looked out at him. "What kind of meal do you have for the condemned?"

Her sarcasm wasn't disguised, but he chose not to respond in kind. Instead he reached for the cell door, slid it shut with a clang of metal against metal and saw her flinch. "How about sandwich and soup?"

She pressed her hands to her knees and shrugged. "Whatever."

She'd get whatever he could manage. He turned to lock the door at the security panel on the opposite wall, but stopped when she spoke again. "Can you leave the door open?"

He looked back at her. "The cells have to be locked so—"

"No, that door," she said, pointing to the lockdown area's metal security door. "Can you just leave that one open for now? Just in case I faint again or something?"

He seemed to be making up the rules as he went along, so he just nodded, hit the lock button and the cell door clicked. Back in his dad's office, Joshua sat at the desk and realized, for the first time, the desk was positioned to view the security door. Riley was pacing in the cell, back and forth, going out of sight, coming back into sight, then going out of sight again.

He grabbed the phone receiver, put in a call to Rusty's Diner and swivelled his chair so it faced the window that overlooked the security yard. Following Gordie's instructions, he ordered a turkey sandwich and soup from the small diner a couple of blocks north of the station, and was told the order would be delivered as soon as they found someone to bring it over to him.

Once he'd hung up, Joshua let his eyes skim over the office. It almost felt like home, with a comfortable sameness to it that had settled over the years. He'd thought filling in for his dad would be a snap. Just do what Charlie needed, give him a break now and then. But in an odd way this place had been his lifeline once he came back.

Now it felt uncomfortable, as if something was hanging over his head, a certain discomfort that he couldn't label. Maybe an uneasiness. He didn't know why. His little girl J.J. was fine, back at the ranch with his dad and his stepmother. Joshua didn't have to be anywhere he didn't want to be. He could walk out of here right now and that would be that. But on a gut level, he wasn't sure why he'd agreed to do this. He was here for the duration, in a ski town whose bitter cold was a far cry from Atlanta, facing the coming holidays with no anticipation beyond getting through them and to the other side, into a new year.

He sat forward, looked down at the papers on the desk and read the top one about a stolen BMW out of Chicago. Handwritten in the margin was "Riley Shaw," along with a notation with the detective's name in Chicago and some other notes. He glanced up and was relieved she wasn't at the cell door any longer.

The radio signaled an incoming call and he hit Receive on the box on his desk. It was Charlie calling in. The incident at the lifts was under control and he was taking Wes with him on rounds, then he'd be back. Joshua would be here for another two hours at least.

He stared at the papers on his desk. Just talking to the detective from Chicago had let him know the case wasn't a priority in any sense of the word. If it took a day or two or even three, they wouldn't sweat it. But if Charlie agreed to hold off on booking, he wouldn't do it more than a day. Two, tops. Joshua had an idea and reached for the phone. He put in a call to Harvey Sills, a cop who'd worked vice in a Chicago suburb for ten years and someone he'd dealt with on a case four years ago.

News was Harvey had taken early retirement after being wounded, but had stayed in the business as a private investigator. He didn't have any trouble getting a number and putting in a call to Harvey. It rang four times, then went to voice mail.

"Harvey. Joshua Pierce, here," he said after the beep. "I know it's been a while, but I'm back in Silver Creek, filling in for my dad for a while. I'm working a case out of the Chicago area and I need some help. I was thinking you might be able to expedite it for me. If you could call me when you get a chance, I'd appreciate it." He left his cell number and the office number, then hung up.

Harvey had contacts and he was right there in the city. If anyone could get answers, he could. The buzzer sounded when the entry door to the station opened, and Joshua got up at the same time someone called from the squad room. "Hey, where is everyone?"

Spotting Annie Logan just rounding the reception desk, Joshua got up and headed out. Annie was the owner of the Silver Creek Hotel, and apparently the delivery service for Rusty's Diner at the moment. She was holding an orange take-out bag in one hand and pushing off her fur-lined hood with the other. She smiled when she saw him. "There you are." She beamed.

He crossed to meet her halfway and realized Annie hadn't changed since they were kids. She'd been plain then, and still was, but somewhere along the way she'd developed a certain attractiveness. She'd always smiled, been happy and full of life. Married and happy, she worked at the hotel she owned with her husband, Rick.

She was grinning at him, her face flushed from the cold. "Boy it seems like old times seeing you in this place." She handed him the bag. "Too bad your dad's not here, too. How's he doing?"

"He's staying out of trouble, getting better," he said.

"Who've you got in there?" she asked, looking around him at the open security door. "I heard you were babysitting a prisoner. Who is it, that Jenner kid? Or some drunk who thought they could ski down Main Street and use the cars as slalom markers?"

"Just a common car thief," he said, realizing how wrong that was as soon as he said it. There was nothing "common" about Riley Shaw.

"Oh, big-time law stuff, huh?" She grinned.

"Yeah," he said. "How much do I owe you?"

"Rusty said he'd put it on the tab. You know, if this is the way you do things, you should forget about going back to Atlanta and run for sheriff here when your dad's term is up. Making big arrests and all. You could give Charlie a run for his money."

That wasn't even in his thought process. He knew he'd go back to Atlanta, but he wasn't sure what he'd

do there. He wasn't at all sure he'd go back to law enforcement. He had options and he was still weighing
them. "Who in their right mind would go up against
Charlie? I wouldn't stand a chance."

Annie patted his arm and said with mock seriousness, "Humility is a good thing, Joshua. A very good
thing."

RILEY COULD HEAR Joshua talking to a woman who
sounded so happy and cheerful that it was almost painful to listen to. "Did you hear it's going to snow tonight?" the woman asked. "Who would have thought
we were all wailing about having no snow not too
long ago?" She laughed for some reason, then asked,
"How's J.J. doing?"

J.J.? His wife? Riley had seen a wedding ring on
his finger.

"She's doing great," he said.

"You give her a big hug for me, you hear?"

"Absolutely."

Her voice was getting farther away as she spoke.
"Say hi to your folks?"

"Absolutely," he said.

"Good to have you back, Josh. See you soon." A
door opened, then closed and there was silence.

Riley pulled the blankets off the cot, threw them
into the left front corner of the cell onto the floor, then
crossed over and sank onto them. She could see out
the security door from here and right into the office
she'd been in earlier. If she stayed on the cot, all she
could see was empty desks. She sat back, resting
against the bars, and looked around the cell. Dull

walls, cement flooring, the spindly cot with its thin mattress, the stark toilet and a sink stuck in the wall. Someone had brought in a corrugated screen that was about four feet high and three feet wide, made of what looked like cardboard. It was supposed to be for some privacy in the toilet area, but all it did was add more ugliness to the space. Even the single window looked stark.

She closed her eyes to shut out her surroundings and pulled up her knees to press her forehead against them. Joshua and that Annie person sounded like friends; old, comfortable friends. They teased a bit, talked about family. And for a moment, she ached with the sense that she didn't have that. She never had. Friends. Family. She closed her eyes so tightly colors exploded behind them. She didn't know much about those things.

"What in the hell?"

Her head jerked up at the sound of Joshua's sharp exclamation and she twisted around to see him inside the lockdown area on the other side of the bars to her cell, staring at her. "What's wrong?" she asked, scrambling to her feet.

He was holding a bright orange bag in one hand, his face set in a dark frown. "I didn't see you there," he said.

She sank back on the blankets and watched him as he crossed to the security panel. He punched in the code and the cell door clicked. He turned, reaching for the cell door and sliding it back. "Oh, I get it. You thought I'd made a break for it, didn't you?"

He didn't look at her as he crossed to the small table by the cot. "I don't know what I thought," he said as he reached into the bag and took out a foam carton and a small covered cup.

"Whatever," she murmured as he turned and crossed to where she was sitting.

"Why are you sitting on the floor?" he asked. "Were you dizzy again or sick or something?"

She had to crane her neck a bit to look up at him. "Just thinking," she said.

"The bed's not too uncomfortable, and I can bring in a chair if you need a place to sit, a place to think."

She shrugged, then brushed at the denim on her legs. "Thanks, but I'm good."

He shook his head, as if he questioned her sanity. "Well, there's hot soup and a sandwich over there when you want it."

She was silent.

He frowned at her. "You know, we can do this the easy way or the hard way. And personally, I prefer the easy way."

"Easy for you," she said, and got quickly to her feet.

Her movement caught him off guard and she accidentally bumped into his shoulder, rocking her backward. He caught her just before she would have struck the bars, and held her with both hands, gripping her shoulders. For a moment they were inches from each other and she could see a flare of gold in his hazel eyes. "Steady?" he asked.

She hadn't felt steady since she'd first heard the siren and seen the flashing lights. "Sure," she lied. "I'm steady."

He hesitated, then let her go, but didn't move back

to give her any space. "Let's make this as easy on both of us as we can, okay?"

"Okay, okay," she said on a sigh. "Coffee sounds lovely if it's convenient for you and you don't have to go out of your way to get it."

"I'll get it," he said, and for a moment she thought he was going to smile. There was something in his eyes, maybe a shadow of humor at his lips. She wasn't sure. "Coffee it is." He crossed to the cell door, then turned back to her. "Cream and sugar?"

"No, thank you very much."

This time he did smile, a quick, quirky expression that took years off his features before it was gone. And he was gone, leaving the cell door standing open. She thought of her crack about making a break for it, and if she'd had any place to go, she might have considered it. But she didn't have anywhere to go.

So she checked on the food—a turkey sandwich on some wheat bread and a small cup with a lid. She opened the cup, found some sort of fragrant vegetable soup, then took it back with her to the corner of the cell and dropped down onto the floor. She sat cross-legged and hardly noticed when Joshua returned.

She didn't look up, but stared at the soup and listened to him cross to the cot. When he came over to her, she glanced at his boots, at the scuffs and obvious wear. They certainly weren't your regulation-issue cop shoes, that was for sure. He cleared his throat and said, "Coffee's on the table."

She expected him to leave, but he didn't. Instead he crouched in front of her. "The easy way is for you to tell me exactly what's going on."

She sighed heavily. "I told you what happened. That's it."

He was silent for a long, nerve-racking moment, then said, "I know what you said, now how about the truth?"

Chapter Four

This time Riley didn't bother to control her reaction. She rolled her eyes and sighed with heavy emphasis. "Oh, is this your bad-cop routine? Getting coffee and food was a good-cop routine?" She could see the anger in him now and she didn't care. "I think I should tell you that it really works better with two people to act it out."

"Very funny," he muttered, but didn't leave.

She'd wanted him to stay, just to have someone else here, but now she wanted him gone. "Tell you what, why don't you go and play some childish game like ding-dong-ditch and leave me alone?"

He still didn't leave. "Listen to me, all I'm trying to do is find out the truth."

"I told you the truth. And the more I think about it, I think I was set up, that I'm the pawn in some huge stolen car ring and you've got the wrong person." She really expected him to either go or to laugh in her face, because she knew she was doing a huge what-if that was even hard for her to buy. "Oh, just forget it," she said, looking back down at the soup that was getting cold.

He still didn't leave. Instead he said, "Not so fast. Stranger things have happened. Being a cop, you see all sorts of weird things."

Her eyes shot back to his. "What?"

He shrugged. "I'm willing to consider anything."

Riley didn't let herself hope for much in her life, she never had, but in that moment she felt the nudging of what she suspected was hope. "And?" she asked.

"I think it's worth looking into."

Riley felt a flutter of hope. He believed her? "You think so? They set me up? Here I've got the car, and if I get stopped, I'm arrested, and if I'm not stopped, they get their car and no one's the wiser?"

"It's happened before," he murmured.

She couldn't read his expression and she desperately wanted to. No, she wanted affirmation that he was starting to take her seriously. "It all makes some weird sense, you know. Maybe that's what happened, or maybe it's just a big misunderstanding. Some weird confusion. Could there be some confusion about the car being stolen, being on the list by mistake?"

He shook his head. "No, that's a fact."

"But you believe me that I didn't steal the car?"

She literally held her breath and the flicker of hope was gone when he shook his head. "No. I told you, I'm willing to consider options. All I know for sure is, the car's stolen and you were driving it."

She sank back against the bars, horrified that it had meant so much to have this man believe even part of what she'd told him. "The facts, ma'am, just the facts."

"That's about it.

"If a friend of yours was caught like I was, and they told you it was all a mix-up, a mistake or some sort of nefarious plot, would you believe him?"

"That isn't the point," he said with unerring logic. But it was for her. He'd believe a friend anytime. Not a stranger. "People let you see what they want you to see."

"Sometimes it has to be the truth."

"In this job, it's usually not."

That drew the lines completely. He was the cop, she was the crook. "Your job stinks."

He didn't take offense. "More times than not," he said as he stood.

She crooked her neck to look up at him, her soup all but forgotten. "Then why do you do it?"

He flexed his shoulders, as if to ease his muscles, and didn't answer her for a moment. At first she thought he was just going to ignore her, then she realized he was thinking. "Good question," was all he said. He looked down at the cup of soup in her hands. "Anything else you need?"

Nothing he could give her. "No."

He left without another word, sliding the cell door shut with a clang. He secured it and walked out, but left the security door open again. She sat back, shifting a bit so that she was in the corner and could see out into the squad room. She watched Joshua cross the space directly to the office. He stopped at the open door, turned back in her direction and, although she was sure he could see her watching him, he didn't acknowledge it. He just went in and sat behind the desk.

She looked away and sipped her tepid soup. If his

job sucked, hers surpassed that derogatory term ten-fold. Drive a car to San Diego. That was it. And this was the end result. She was startled to hear voices in the next room. Male voices. She looked in that direction and saw nothing at first, then two uniforms passed her line of sight so quickly she couldn't recognize them. When they went into Joshua's office, she saw that it was the man Joshua had said was the acting sheriff, Charlie, and another shorter man she'd never seen before.

She watched them through the upper glass windows of the office wall. Joshua remained seated behind the desk, the other two stood with their backs to her. She couldn't see what was going on, until Joshua stood and came around to face the other two. He was talking to Charlie while the other man looked as if he was standing at attention, observing. Charlie was shaking his head emphatically as Joshua moved closer and kept talking.

When Charlie glanced in her direction, Riley knew they were talking about her. The deal. Waiting for the booking. And from the looks of it, Charlie wasn't having any part of it. Then Joshua touched the man on his shoulder and got his attention again. The two kept talking, and finally Joshua moved back. Charlie turned and left the office. Riley couldn't tell a thing from either man's expression.

Charlie was out of sight to the right and Joshua was saying something to the other man who had just removed his uniform cap. From a distance he looked very blond, with a buzz cut and a florid face. He simply listened, giving no real response that she could make out. Then the blond left, heading in the same direction as Charlie. Joshua went back to his desk and sat, never looking in her direction.

Riley could feel that there was bad news coming. Charlie wasn't about to let this slide. So she'd be booked. She heard a door open and close, more voices that were too indistinct to make out, the sound of a keyboard being used, then, jarringly, a Christmas carol came through ceiling speakers.

She heard another door open and close, but Joshua never looked up from the desk. "Yeah, I got to stay," someone said loudly enough to be heard over the music. Possibly Charlie. He sounded as if he was pretty close to the open door. "I'll try to get out of here in an hour or two. You go ahead to the party and I'll catch up with you."

She saw Joshua stand and move out of sight. He never looked her way before disappearing, wearing his heavy coat. Charlie approached the security door and blocked her view.

"How are you doing?" He looked pretty casual for an acting sheriff, his uniform shirt open at the neck and his hat gone.

"Okay," she murmured.

He entered the lockdown area, touching the bars of her cell door with his left hand. He wore a plain gold wedding band. "Why are you on the cold, hard floor?"

She wasn't about to explain how she could breathe better sitting here, or how she could more easily see what was going on outside. "I'm eating some soup," she said, lifting the cup with its barely touched contents.

"Joshua told me what he wants to do with your case, and I can't say I agree," he said, and she knew she'd been right. This wasn't good news. "Booking you is the thing to do."

She got to her feet and faced him through the bars. "He said you could maybe wait a day or so, just until Chicago verifies my story."

He shook his head. "I know what he told you, and I don't like it."

She didn't realize until that moment how much she'd counted on Joshua being able to deliver, to come through for her. "The rules are the rules, huh?"

"Always have been and always will be, but I told him I'd let him run with this, at least for another day."

Relief came in a rush. "Oh, thank you."

"Oh, I'm not doing it for you, Miss Shaw, not even for Joshua, not really. But his father, he's been a real friend, and a great sheriff, so out of respect for him, I'll let it slide." He still looked grim. "But if you're just giving us the runaround, there'll be hell to pay."

The threat hung between them and she didn't doubt that behind Charlie's good-old-boy exterior, he'd be the one to deliver the consequences in person. "I'm innocent," she said.

"Miss, everyone who's been in here's been innocent. Even the guy last week who decided to rearrange his friend's face with a ski pole. He was innocent. He never even touched the pole, or so he told me." He motioned toward the cot. "The bed's made for sleeping and sitting," he said. With that, he turned to head for the security door.

"Sir?" she said when he reached for the handle to

pull the door shut behind him. "Can you leave the door open?"

He glanced back at her. "Sure. Don't want you to fall and hit your head or something. Do you need more blankets or pillows for the night?"

"Yes, please," she said.

He left and the door stayed open. "Thanks," she whispered to the nothingness around her as she slowly sank to the floor. Pressing her back to the bars, the soup all but forgotten, she looked at the single window set high in the cell wall. Wire mesh in the glass distorted it, but she could see it was dark outside. Night. She'd been here longer than she'd realized.

"Here you go," Charlie said as he came back with an armload of blankets and two pillows. He punched in the security code, then pulled back the cell door and entered, crossing to drop them on the cot. He turned and came over to her, frowning. "Anything else?"

"Let me out?"

His bark of laughter echoed in the space around them. "Now that I can't do." He crossed to the cell door and stepped out, closing it behind him with a solid thud. He went through the routine of setting the security code before he twisted a switch on the wall and the lights dimmed. They went from a stark glare to a softness that she really welcomed. Things looked less bleak now, less dreary and cold. When he left, the security door stayed open.

Riley stayed where she was for a long time, then she slowly got up and headed for the cot. She was here for the night, so she'd better accept it. She put the soup on the table, then picked up a blanket, shook it out, wrapped it around her and lay on the bed. She could hear every noise from the next room; the footsteps, the continuous music, voices that were low, the crackle of a two-way radio.

She'd been fifteen the last time she was in a cell. Fifteen and terrified. She'd gone on a joyride with three of the kids she'd met on the streets when she'd walked out of her last foster home, and the police had stopped them almost immediately. Two of the kids had been handed over to the their parents, but she and a skinny kid with a purple mohawk had stayed behind.

The boy had been transferred and she'd never seen him again. She'd been detained in the juvenile section for two weeks before she'd finally seen a judge. Two weeks of being locked up and locked down, and by the time she'd been taken in front of the judge, she'd figured she was lost.

Thankfully she'd been wrong. She'd been handed her life back. Given a chance to get an education, to make something of herself, to work toward a future, and she had done that very thing. Until now. Now she was back in a cell and there wasn't going to be another chance given to her if she couldn't prove she was innocent.

She stared at the wall, restless and unable to relax. She tried relaxation breathing to put herself to sleep. Sleep was an escape of sorts. She couldn't go anywhere physically, but she could ignore this place and drift off. She tried, over and over, and just when she thought she'd never sleep again, she felt the tug of slumber and she gave in to it.

She left the jail cell and fell into welcome blackness. Soft. Quiet. Blackness. But as she drifted, she sensed something. Someone. She wasn't alone. Someone was with her, so close she could feel the warmth of exhaled breath on her skin. She could move and touch the presence; she could have a connection, an anchor. There was no fear or even surprise at the presence. Somewhere, deep in her soul, she'd expected it and relished the sense of not being alone.

But the good feelings started to dissolve when she reached out and touched no one. They were there, but she couldn't find them. She couldn't reach them. Panic came in a rush as she frantically reached out. But she fell back, back, back and as she slipped into a dreamless sleep, she caught a glimpse of the presence floating away from her.

She had a flashing image. Joshua Pierce. He watched her, had a hand out to her, but the chasm between them was insurmountable. Their hands never touched, never made that connection. He moved farther away. And she'd been wrong. He wasn't her hope. He wasn't anything. Then he was gone, hope was gone, and she was alone.

JOSHUA HAD AVOIDED the station last night and most of today. When he'd finally agreed to cover a shift, it was the midnight-to-eight shift. The "dead dog" shift, as Charlie called it. He'd spent the day at the ranch with J.J. and his dad, and he'd called in twice to find out what Chicago had said. Nothing. No word at all. Harvey Sills had returned his call, taken the information and told him he'd do what checking he could on Riley Shaw and the names he'd been given. There was nothing else Joshua could do, and the twenty-four hours he'd pried out of Charlie before booking her were coming to an end.

Colin, a local kid who'd decided to become a policeman, had just graduated from the academy and had left on patrol with Todd, so Joshua settled in for the night. The nights weren't easy for him since Sarah's death, so staying busy was a good thing. At least, it always had been.

He closed things down, turned off the annoying Christmas music someone had cranked up, ignored the foil Christmas tree Charlie's wife, Walleen, had put up on the reception desk, and finally knew he had to go in to see Riley Shaw. He didn't realize until he looked in the door to the lockdown area that he'd stayed away because of her. He hadn't wanted to tell her there was nothing from Chicago, and if Wes's version of her reaction when he'd told her was any example of what she would have done, he was glad he hadn't been the bearer of bad news. According to the deputy, she'd been completely still, letting him just get out of the cell and close the door before she kicked her lunch across the space.

Now she was quiet, lying on the cot on her side, a blanket twisted around her, her feet bare and her hair loose and caught in a tangle of auburn against the starkness of the pillows. He moved closer to the bars and he could hear her soft breathing, an odd mumble here and there. No, he hadn't wanted to give her the bad news or to listen to her stories about car theft rings and wonder why in the world he wanted to believe her. He usually didn't have any vested interest in a prisoner's guilt or innocence. The facts were the facts. Plain and simple.

But with Riley Shaw, he found himself wondering what he could do to fix things, to get this over and done with, to let her go. He'd even gone up against Charlie, something he would never have thought of doing before. And he knew he was going to try to buy more time if nothing showed up in the morning. He'd talk to Charlie, get a hold of Harvey, connect with Detective Gagne in Chicago, and maybe something would turn up.

She moaned softly and shifted, one hand lifting to reach out into the air as if she were trying to find something. Then slowly it lowered back to the gray blanket, closing into a loose fist. He turned away and left, not about to figure out why he was so intent on giving her every chance he could to prove her innocence.

He headed back to the office and the night stretched out in front of him, so he pulled paperwork and got busy. They couldn't do anything with Riley until morning, so he tried to push her out of his mind. Hopefully he'd feel tired soon, stretch out on the couch in the office and maybe, if he was very lucky, he'd get some real sleep.

He realized he'd looked at the same supply-request form for five minutes without doing a thing about it before he tossed the sheet of paper onto the pile on his desk. As he sat back, he heard a noise that caught his attention. He frowned, not sure what it was. He looked up at the clock. Midnight. He listened and it came again. Soft and muffled, it sounded almost like a trapped animal.

He got up and hurried out of the office, looked around at the empty squad room, then realized it was coming from the cell area. He ran past the desks, through the open security door and barely noticed the pile of blankets in a tangle on the floor when he spotted Riley. She was on the bed, facedown, stretched out, her body shaking, her hair a mass of tangled curls and her hands clutching the pillows she had her face buried in. A seizure? A fit?

He quickly hit the security panel and rushed into the cell. He grabbed her by the shoulders and everything stopped. The noise, her breathing. He pulled sharply to flip her over onto her back. Pillows scattered as she landed flat on the cot, and he was over her, half on the cot, ready for anything.

What he saw stopped him dead with one knee on the cot, his other foot braced on the floor and his hands pressed flat to the mattress on either side of her body at her shoulders. He looked down at her, into huge blue eyes, her flushed skin, her lips parted in surprise. He heard her take a rough gulp of air before she grabbed at his arms, trying to push him away as she twisted to her right and back toward the wall.

She scooted to the stone, her face partially hidden by the veil of hair that had been loosed from its restraint. But he could see her eyes as she sat cross-legged and stared at him. "What in the heck were you trying to do?" she gasped.

Save your life, he thought, but bit back that response as he moved off the cot to stand. The muscles in his neck were tight; he knew his nerves were on edge for a variety of reasons tonight. But this woman was definitely near the top of the list, her and her fake seizure. "What were you doing, pretending you were having a seizure or something?"

"No," she muttered as she raked her hair back from her face with both hands.

For a split second she looked painfully vulnerable. Despite the annoyance in her voice, she was frightened, and he could see a pulse beating wildly at her throat where the top three buttons of her shirt had come undone.

His nerves tensed even more. "Then what was it?"

She let go of her hair and it fell around her shoulders, with one strand falling softly on her cheek. He closed both hands into fists and pushed them behind his back when he felt an impulse to reach out and brush it away from her flushed skin. "Okay, okay, I was screaming," she said on a theatrical sigh.

"What?"

"Screaming, as in sucking in a lot of air and letting it out as loudly as you can, over and over again?"

"I know what screaming is. The question is why?"

She tucked the strand behind her ear as she shrugged. "Wouldn't you be screaming if you were locked up for something you didn't do and..." She paused. "No one believed you? No one gave a damn?"

He shouldn't give a damn, but, truth be told, he knew he did. And he didn't need that. He reached down and picked up one of the fallen pillows, then tossed it at her. "Knock yourself out."

She ignored the pillow and frowned. If looks could kill, he'd be six feet under. "All heart, aren't you?" she muttered.

That struck a painful nerve, because he wasn't at all sure he even had a heart anymore. "I never claimed to be," he countered tightly.

She grabbed the pillow and held it out to him now. "Here, be my guest. You look as if you could use a good scream."

He thought screaming had a certain allure at that moment, but he ignored the pillow. "Who taught you to do that?"

She pulled the pillow back and hugged it. "Some psychologist I saw a long time ago. He said if you scream, you let go of something, or produce something, maybe an endorphin or something like that, and it helps you relax and refocus. It's sort of like crying, but it works better and doesn't leave you with ugly, puffy red eyes."

He doubted anything could make her eyes ugly, but he'd guarantee that crying didn't do anything to help you focus or relax. "Are you done screaming?"

"For now," she said, tossing the pillow down beside her on the cot. "But you know what?"

He didn't have a clue. "No, what?"

"I'm hungry. That Todd person brought me my dinner, and it was some horrible chili that was so hot it was inedible. He took it away and he never brought me anything else." She brushed at her shirt. "And these are the same clothes I've been wearing for—" She shrugged. "For forever, and taking a bird bath in that tiny sink is getting ridiculous."

"Anything else on your list?" he asked.

"What about Chicago? Surely they called or faxed or sent a homing pigeon by now?"

He shook his head. "No, nothing. This sort of thing

can take time, especially at this time of year." He could have walked out, shut the cell and gone back to his office, but he didn't. "I can't do a thing about Chicago right now, since it's late, but I might be able to find you something to snack on."

He started to turn to go hunt down something for her, but she startled him when she scooted off the cot and grabbed his arm to stop him from leaving. He turned to her. "Charlie's going to book me in the morning."

She was inches from him and he knew he hadn't avoided anything by staying away today. Those blue eyes were on him, half accusatory and half expectant. "I expected he might," he said.

"Can't you do something about it?" She didn't let go of him and he didn't miss the increasing tightness in her hold. "You talked him into holding off before. Can't you do it again?"

How did she know what he'd done before? "I just suggested it might be a good thing to hold off for a day."

"But he did it, and if you ask, he might do it again." She was so close he felt the air stir when she moved even closer. "Please, you have to. I'll do anything if you do."

He stared down into her eyes, at her mouth, softly parted, and thought of images of what "anything" implied. It left heat in its path, and he knew in that split second how alone he'd been in the eighteen months since Sarah died. His emotions were scrambled and distorted. Standing in a jail cell with a suspected car thief, he was feeling things that made no sense at all.

He pulled away from her touch and narrowed his

eyes. Anger at himself filled his voice when he said, "Do you want 'bribing an officer' to be added to your charges?"

She was still for a long moment, then she actually laughed at him, a soft sound that permeated the air around him. "You think that I was offering to—" She bit her lip. "Sir, I just meant that I'd be grateful for any help you can give me. I wasn't implying…" Her color deepened, but the smile didn't fade completely. "You're wrong, dead wrong. Just the way you've been about me from the start."

He regrouped, trying to focus. He'd thought so many things in just a few flashing moments, and he'd been dead wrong, just the way she said. His nerves tightened to the point of pain and he twisted his head to try to ease the tension. "Sure, dead wrong," he muttered, turning away from her. This time she didn't stop him with her touch, but with her words.

"The food?"

"Sure," he said over his shoulder without stopping or looking back at her.

"And clean clothes and a hot shower while you're at it?"

He kept walking, saying, "Right now, it's food." Then he was out of the cell, not bothering to lock it, and through the security door, out of her reach. At least for now.

Chapter Five

Riley was horrified at what he thought she'd been offering, and it took everything she had to force a laugh. The assumption and the fact that he hadn't even questioned it, stung. She'd been very close to begging him for his help, but when he'd responded like that, she knew she wouldn't try it again. She stared at the empty doorway, waiting for him to come back.

He didn't look much like a cop tonight, in a forest-green flannel shirt, jeans and walking boots, but he sure acted like one. She dropped down onto the cot, scooted back, folded her legs yoga-style and rested her hands palms up on her knees. She let her head drop back, closed her eyes and touched her thumbs and middle fingers together to form an "O" before slowly rotating her head in circles. "Ooohhhmmmm," she chanted over and over again on a whisper.

"What are you doing now?"

His voice startled Riley and her body tensed as her eyes flew open. Joshua Pierce stood in front of her, holding a box of crackers and a couple of snack bars in one hand and a heavy ceramic mug in the other. "I was trying to relax," she said, taking the mug when he offered it to her.

"Does it help?" he asked.

She cradled the mug in both hands and sipped some of the steamy coffee. It was a lot better than the stuff they'd brought to her earlier. She looked up at him over the mug. "Sometimes it helps." She sipped more coffee and felt compelled to tell him that she had never meant to offer herself to him in exchange for his help.

"Before, when you thought… When I said that to you, I wasn't suggesting anything criminal." He watched her, letting her do all the talking, and it was making her more and more uncomfortable. "I mean, I suppose you've had that happen before, with the way some people think and all, but I never meant that. Not ever."

All he said was, "Sure," which did nothing to make her feel better.

She spoke in a rush. "I'm so grateful for what you've already done. Charlie let me know he never would have waited if it hadn't been for you asking."

"He didn't fight it too much."

"He said he did it mostly for your dad, but if you hadn't asked, he wouldn't have thought about doing it at all. That was really good of you. Thanks."

"Sure," he said again. He put the box of crackers and the snack bars on the bed. "There you go," he said, and turned to leave. He was going to walk out, lock the door, and she'd be totally alone again. So she spoke up. She'd say anything to keep him around for a few minutes more.

"So you're filling in now until someone else comes in to do the night shift?"

He shrugged. "No, I'm here all night while the others do their rounds."

"I didn't think you were really working." She glanced at his clothes. "That's not a uniform."

"I don't have a real uniform. I'm temporary, so there is no reason to get one." She remembered that even when he'd arrested her, the jacket had been part of a uniform, with badges and all, and the "trooper" hat, but she hadn't really noticed the rest. Maybe the shirt had been a plain long-sleeved one? She wasn't sure. "And doing the late shift, you don't have to be so formal."

He could talk to prisoners and bring them coffee and snacks. During the day she'd had a hard time getting anyone's attention, let alone getting anyone to bring her coffee and things. She picked up one of the bars and tore off the wrapper. She studied the compressed nuts and fruit that looked decidedly dry and unappetizing.

"Thanks for getting this for me," she said, and tried a taste. She stopped at one nibble, quickly took a drink of coffee to wash it down, then put her coffee mug back in the crook of her knee. "Wow, I bet this is good for me. Isn't that the case, that if it tastes terrible, it has to be good for you, and if it tastes great, it's bad for you?"

"I think I've heard that," he said. "Try dunking it in your coffee. Maybe that'll help."

She took his advice, tasted the bar and smiled. "It's almost edible."

She thought that he was going to smile, but it never happened. In the low lights, he studied her for a moment, then said, "Do you need anything else?"

She spoke quickly and honestly. "Company." He wasn't going to stay. He was ready to bolt, and she said quickly, "In case I faint or get sick."

"Just lie down on the cot and try to sleep. If you can't, count the stones in the wall. They're even-numbered, by the way."

"Excuse me?"

"The stones are even-numbered. If you start at the top in the corner and go across, there are as many horizontally as there are vertically."

She dropped the bar on the torn wrapper by her side and studied him. "How do you know that, unless you've..." She chuckled as she realized something. "Unless you've been locked up in a cell here?" She didn't miss his slight grimace at her words. "Interesting. Very interesting," she murmured.

"No, it's not," he said quickly, one hand held toward her, palm out. "Not at all."

"Oh, come on, spill the beans. You've been locked up here, haven't you? Let me guess why you were arrested. You were going the wrong way on a ski run? Or you ditched school to build snowmen?" She lowered her voice conspiratorially. "Come on, you can tell me. I'll understand."

He laughed and the sound and expression were so unexpected that they literally stopped her breath for a second or two. "Oh, you will, will you?"

"Sure, one con to another." And she found a smile herself, a real smile, and it was such a relief to be able to smile at all. "Come on. Come clean."

He shook his head. "Forget it. It's too late to do this. I need to get to work."

"Oh, don't go." She didn't want to sound desperate, but she could almost hear it in her words. "Get yourself some of this delicious coffee and stay awhile. I promise I won't pry into your reprobate past. To be honest, I just hate this time of night and…" She shrugged. "You're awake and I'm awake."

She hadn't meant to say anything about the night to him. He wasn't a kindred spirit. That wasn't likely. But she wanted him to stay to keep the night at bay for just a bit longer. She didn't want to get so lonely and so scared and so angry again that she'd bury her face in the pillows and scream herself hoarse. And meditating wouldn't do a bit of good. "Can't you take a coffee break?"

She waited, the world at a standstill until he finally nodded and said, "Sure. I'll be right back."

He left and returned in less than a minute with a straight-backed wooden chair and a cup of coffee. He sat facing her on the cot. All she could do was smile in relief. He took a quick drink of his coffee, coughed slightly, then sat back in the chair, the coffee mug resting on his thigh.

Now he was here, she didn't know what to say. She kept thinking about the stones. Why not? "So how many stones are there both ways?"

He motioned to the wall where it met the ceiling in the left corner of her cell. "Start there and count. You'll find out that there are exactly nineteen stones across and nineteen stones down. Then take out the window space and you can get the total."

"How long did it take for you to figure that out?"

"One night."

"Oh, I was right. One night, huh?"

"Don't look too impressed," he said, cupping the mug in both hands. "I wasn't any Al Capone or anything."

She reached for the crackers, opened the box and held it out to him. "Help yourself."

He waved aside the crackers, then sat forward, resting his elbows on his knees. "No, thanks."

She put the cracker box down, then picked up the power bar again. "Okay, so the cop's kid was put in jail?"

"Yes."

She dunked the bar in her coffee, then nibbled the end off. "Your dad kept the law, so it behooved you to break it. So what did you do?"

"Nothing great. Not much more than the ding-dong-ditch game you mentioned."

"You knew what that was?" she asked, the bar halfway to her mouth when it stopped.

"Sure. You find a house, ring the bell and run like hell?"

She dunked the bar and bit off more of it, finding it almost palatable if she kept it soggy with warm coffee. "So your dad locked you up for that?"

He took a sip of his own coffee, then said, "No. He got me for something else, and he let the deputies deal with me. He thought it would do me good to find out what it was like to be locked up. An object lesson of sorts."

"And did it work?"

"I ended up being a cop," he said. "So I guess it worked, and I sure like the outside better than the inside."

The humor was failing her now. "Who wouldn't?" she murmured, looking at the half-finished bar in her hand.

Joshua watched her closely and saw the easy teasing that had been going on between them fading away. He'd relaxed, able to forget a lot of things, but as her humor died, he wished he could get her to smile again. But he was clean out of jokes of any sort. "Yeah, who wouldn't?"

She took a deep breath, released it slowly, and he just bet that was another of her relaxation techniques. "So you got out and moved to Atlanta and joined the force?" she finally asked.

"Not exactly. I was here for a while working with Dad, then got a job offer in Atlanta and..." He shrugged. "As they say, the rest is history."

"But you came back here."

"Yeah." He took another sip of coffee, letting the hot liquid slide down his throat.

She cocked her head to one side, and said, "I'm not trying to be nosy, but why did you come back?"

Since Riley wasn't a violent offender, Joshua figured someone would have told her why he was here. He'd been the hot topic of gossip since he'd come home. First him being a widower, then being an eligible man again. He hated both tags. He gave her a bare-bones explanation. "I'm filling in for my dad, to help with a manpower shortage they had when he had a heart attack and couldn't work. Charlie stepped up to fill in as acting sheriff, and I fill in where they need me. It makes Dad rest easier if he isn't worried about them being short-handed at the holidays."

"Is your father okay?" she asked with what sounded like genuine concern.

"He's recovering." Why would she look relieved that his father was healing? "He's tough and stubborn."

"Good. That's a good trait when it comes to fighting anything." She sipped some of her coffee, secured the mug again, then asked more questions. "So you and your wife are here?"

He'd heard of people "flinching inside," but he'd never understood exactly what that meant until that moment. The flinch was made even more painful because of what he'd thought earlier about Riley, that basic response he'd felt in this woman's presence, and now, the mention of Sarah and the fact that he knew right then that Sarah hadn't been in his thoughts very much in the past twenty-four hours. His thoughts had been centered on Riley and her problems.

He'd been thinking about Riley's case, then he'd been in here talking to Riley, watching her, wondering about her. God, the guilt was there, hard and sure. And he tried to cushion himself from it as quickly as he could. "I was in transition with my job," he said. He wasn't going to talk about Sarah, not here, not now. He didn't realize his free hand had closed into a fist where it rested on his thigh until he felt his wedding band cutting into his skin. He eased the clenching. "It's getting late," he said.

"Thanks for keeping me company. I don't know what it is, but the nights are so…" She shrugged, as if she couldn't find the right word before she looked back down into her coffee.

"Empty?"

Her gaze met his and he saw total understanding in them. "Yes, empty," she said.

The moment she echoed the word, he had the thought that in a perfect world Riley Shaw wouldn't hate the night, wouldn't know about that emptiness he'd found with Sarah gone. Riley would be held and loved in the night. And that flinch he'd felt moments ago was there again when he had a ridiculous snap of jealousy for a man in the future who would probably do that very thing. The man who would hold and love Riley for all the future nights of her life. He stood so quickly that the chair's legs screeched on the floor.

She got to her feet a second later. At first he was aware of the way she stirred the air around him, the way it brushed across his face, then he looked down at her. In the half light her eyes were shadowed by long lashes and her expression was effectively muffled. They were toe-to-toe, mere inches separated them, and he studied her, from the lifted chin, the soft lips, the sweep of her throat, the hair resting in a veil around her shoulders. If he narrowed his eyes and blurred the background, things could appear so differently to him. But the stone walls, the cement floors and the bars were reality. Her reality and his, too.

No narrowing of his eyes would change the fact that she was a prisoner, a stranger he knew next to nothing about. He was too damn lonely, and if he didn't leave, the odds were pretty good that he'd do something really stupid. He couldn't risk it. He wouldn't risk it.

RILEY COULD literally see Joshua Pierce shutting down. Whatever ease there had been for a few precious

moments, moments when she could pretend that they
were two people just talking, were gone, and he was
leaving. She glanced down and saw him flex his left
hand and the glint from his wedding band caught in
the low light. She'd noticed it before, but for the time
he'd been in here with her, she hadn't thought of it.
Not even when he'd said how empty the nights were.
"It's late. I have to get back to work."

She looked down and thought, Damn it all, and the
next instant she was startled by his touch, his hand
cupping her chin, lifting her face so she had no choice
but to meet his eyes. "Damn what?" he asked.

She'd said that out loud? She could feel the fire in her
face and his touch rattled her even more. "Damn...
everything," she breathed, and moved her head, breaking the contact so she could think clearly again. "Damn
Chicago and Alvin Nyland and whoever Mindy Sullivan is." His eyes were narrowing with each word.
"Damn you," she said, then realized that time she'd
thought it. She hadn't said it. And she didn't mean it. The
man had family and a life, and she was nothing to him
but a possible car thief. "Damn," she whispered out loud.

"That about covers everything, doesn't it?"

She closed her eyes and wished that screaming in
a pillow would help her right now. It didn't cover the
panic she felt at him leaving her in the cell. It didn't
cover the emptiness that was closing in around her
again. "Sure," she muttered, and turned away, barely
getting her coffee mug to the table before she let go
of it. She reached for the blankets and the pillows and
pushed past Joshua to go to her corner.

"Oh, for Pete's sake," he muttered as she tossed

them on the floor, then sank on top of them. "Use the cot. Scream in your pillow. But do it on the cot."

She grabbed a pillow and pulled it to her middle, but she didn't look up at him. "Go to work," she said, and closed her eyes tightly. She heard his footsteps, the cell door clanging shut after him, the beep of the security code being set, then more footsteps fading away.

She was alone. She buried her head in the pillow she clutched and almost wished she could cry. But her eyes were dry. She'd found out a long time ago that crying didn't help anything. She tried to breathe and to think reasonably. He had work to do. He had a life. He had a wife. Maybe kids. A dad who needed him. Everything she had was in a car they claimed was stolen, and she might not even see that again.

Riley wasn't sure when she laid down in the tangle of blankets and pillows, or when she finally slept, but the next thing she knew, she woke to the thin light of early morning coming in through the single high window over the cot. A phone rang in the distance. Christmas music was being piped in again, and the air felt chilly. She sat up in her corner, stretched, grimaced at the clothes she'd worn for way too long, then grabbed a blanket to pull it around her like a shawl.

She was startled by the sound of a woman calling out from the other room, "Hey, Joshua!" She didn't think it was Annie. "Are you here?"

Riley looked out the open security door and at first didn't see anything, then a woman stepped into her line of sight. At last, she crossed it. In the quick view Riley got, she noticed the woman was short, dressed in heavy outer clothes and a bright pink ski hat, and she was walking quickly. Then she came back into sight, almost to the door of Joshua's office. Now the jacket was gone and from the back, Riley could see she had a slim, girlish figure in a white pullover, jeans and heavy boots trimmed with fur. She skimmed off the pink knit hat, exposing light brown hair, cut in a short, feathery cap.

The woman approached the office door, hesitated, then, looking to the left, said something as she stepped inside. She closed the door behind her. Riley stood to watch her through the upper-office windows. She looked to her left, then headed in that direction and out of sight again. Riley kicked the blankets away from her legs and moved closer to the bars, never taking her eyes off the window wall in the office. Was this Joshua's wife?

The woman strode into sight again, turned back the way she'd come, threw her hands up in the air in an obvious gesture of exasperation, said something, then went to the door. She was out in the next room, leaving the door to the office open after her, and she was heading in a direct line for the lockdown area. Riley grabbed the bar with her right hand, almost bracing herself for some sort of impact.

As the woman approached, Riley realized she was older than she'd first thought. She wasn't in her thirties or forties, but possibly in her fifties or even sixties. Her figure was girlish, but her face showed age— and anger. She wasn't happy. She walked quickly, almost to the open lockdown area door, then she stopped in her tracks, closed her eyes and took a couple of deep breaths. She was squaring herself, settling down. Then she opened her eyes and headed into the cell area.

The minute she saw Riley, her face softened and a lovely smile formed. "Hi, there," she said, crossing to the bars and glancing at the pillows and blankets on the floor. "So is there a shortage of beds around these parts?"

"No, of course not."

"I'm Geneva, but everyone calls me Gen. And I'm here to make sure you get what you need."

"Such as?" she asked a bit leerily.

"Such as a shower and change of clothes, and food. It is a pure shame the way they've let things go."

"You're a prisoner advocate?"

She laughed. "No, I'm Geneva Pierce, the sheriff's wife, and when I heard that this was going on—" She glanced past Riley and took in the small space. "Well, I just had to come on down and fix it. Joshua said it's okay, and even if he hadn't, I'd still do it. Now, you're Riley Shaw, and Joshua has sent a deputy over to the car to get your bags, and as soon as they're cleared, you can have a shower and change your clothes. You'll feel remarkably better, believe me."

"Sure," she said.

Gen eyed her for a long moment. "Joshua tells me that they think you stole a car."

"I didn't."

"That's what Joshua said you'd said."

"What did I say?" Joshua asked as he came into the room carrying her duffel bag.

He looked as tired as she felt. He could use a shower,

too, she thought. The beginnings of a beard shadowed his jaw and, in the thin light, deep lines etched at his mouth.

Gen ignored Joshua's question. "That was fast," she said, and reached for the bag.

"Charlie already had it in impound. I didn't know."

"Great, now open the door so this poor thing can get out and get cleaned up."

Joshua crossed to enter the security code and Gen pulled the door open. She motioned Riley out, and she didn't have to ask twice. When Riley stepped out, Joshua turned without a word and left. Gen touched Riley on the arm. "Come on, dear. Let's get this going."

Riley went with the older woman into the outer room and crossed to the restrooms. She stepped into the women's room and Gen made her way to a door at the far side. Gen grabbed the handle and opened it. "This isn't the best accommodations, but the water's hot and you'll have privacy."

Riley followed her and looked into a room that was barely six-by-six, all done in sterile gray tiles, with three showerheads coming out of the back wall. A community shower room. Riley had seen them before, but never one this small. "There's soap on the shelf," she said, pointing to a tiled ridge between the showerheads. "And—" Gen dug into the pocket of her jeans and brought out two foil packets. "I grabbed these. They're from when Joshua's dad and I went to Las Vegas a while back. Shampoo and rinse." She smiled at Riley. "I tend to take those little toiletries from the hotel rooms."

Riley took them and saw the name of a casino emblazoned in gold on the foil. The Dream Catcher Hotel and Casino. She'd never heard of it, but then again, she'd never been to Las Vegas. "Thanks," she said as Gen put her duffel bag on the lower of two wooden shelves by the door. The top shelf held thin, white folded towels.

"Towels are there," she said. "Just take your time. Have a nice hot shower and things will look a lot better when you're done."

Gen stepped out and quietly closed the door. Riley quickly stripped off her clothes, tossed them on the floor by the door, then turned on the middle shower-head and in moments, steamy hot water cascaded all around her. She stood under it for a very long time, so long in fact that Gen rapped on the door and called, "Everything okay in there?"

"Fine, just fine," Riley replied, and quickly shampooed her hair. In a couple of minutes she had a towel around her head and was digging through her bag for a fresh change of clothes. She noticed that only clothes were in it, none of her personal things, not even a brush.

She dressed in a pair of jeans, an old sweatshirt with her college logo on it, and didn't bother with socks. She toweled her hair, used her fingers to comb it into a semblance of order and knew that a hair dryer wouldn't be one of the perks of the Silver Creek jail. Since her makeup was gone, she was done. She stuffed her old clothes in her duffel, then finally stepped into the restroom.

Gen was half sitting on the edge of the nearest sink and she stood when Riley came out. "My theory is, no matter what a person's done, they deserve a hot shower," she said with a grin as she glanced at Riley's hair. "And a hairbrush."

"I'd appreciate it," she said.

Gen led the way back out into the main office and Riley followed, carrying her duffel with her. "Done?" someone asked, and she knew it was Joshua.

"For now," Gen said as Riley came up beside her.

Joshua held papers rolled into a cylinder in his hand. "Did you get something from Chicago?" she asked.

He shook his head. "No, nothing." He cleared his throat, then said, "Charlie's playing Santa at the town pageant and he'll be out of the office all day."

Riley went closer to him. "All day?"

"All day," he murmured, and she smiled.

"The acting sheriff playing Santa, now isn't that nice?"

Gen looked from Joshua to Riley, then back at Joshua. "And you're delivering this news because…?"

"I just thought you'd like to know."

"He's not coming in?"

When Joshua nodded and said, "Not at all. I'm going to cover for him later on," Riley thought if Gen hadn't been here, she would have done a happy dance right then and there, with wet hair and bare feet. With Charlie busy all day, he couldn't force her arraignment. Then she met Joshua's gaze and she knew that the impulse to do a happy dance was drowned out by the impulse to hug Joshua and to never let go.

Chapter Six

Riley felt Gen touch her arm, and she realized she'd been staring at Joshua. She didn't do any dance or reach out to hug him. She just said, "Thank you," and went with Gen into the lockdown area. As soon as she stepped through the cell door she realized things had changed. Gone was the makeshift cardboard screen in the corner of the room. It had been replaced by a white sheet that hung from pipes. The curtain provided more privacy than the cardboard, and Riley was confused.

"What's this?" she asked, touching the soft cotton.

"I told them that the cardboard was cruel and unusual punishment, and that they'd better replace it with something more…appropriate," Gen said. "Now, you eat and I'll get you some coffee."

While Gen went to get the drink, Riley set her duffel on the floor by the cot and pushed it underneath with her toe. Then she opened the food container to find scrambled eggs, bacon, country potatoes and wheat toast. She hadn't thought she could eat anything, but suddenly she was famished.

She sat down on the cot and ate. By the time Gen returned with the coffee, Riley was half done with the meal. She thanked her, then kept eating.

"Isn't it amazing how a good shower makes food taste better?"

Riley smiled up at Gen. "Thanks for doing all of this. I'm sure it's not in your job description."

"When you live in a small town, or what used to be a small town, you do a lot of double duty. Now, I have to run."

"Thanks," she repeated. Today they'd find out the truth. They had to, she told herself. Today she'd leave this place and head to San Diego, to her new job and her new life. She kept telling herself that, over and over again, but that didn't make it happen.

Joshua had obviously left, and the deputies came and went. The subject of her booking never came up. In the late afternoon, Wes told her he'd check to see if anything had come in, then came back and said succinctly, "Nothing."

It was just after five and through the window she could see the light of day fading. Then she thought she heard Joshua's voice in the other room. Riley stood and tried to see out the open door, but if he was here, he never came into her line of sight. When the Christmas music snapped on a few minutes later, she gave up trying to make out the voices.

A little while later, she saw the blond cop, and got his attention.

The officer stopped in midstride, turned and approached the cell. "Yes, ma'am?" He was short, not more than five-feet-six or so, muscular, with the neck of a bull and pale hair cut so short that it was just a spiked bristle on his scalp. "What do you need?"

"Is Officer Pierce here?"

"No, ma'am, he's not."

She must have imagined his voice. "Do you know if there's been any word from Chicago?"

"Nothing so far, ma'am, but the acting sheriff's out for the day and the others are busy at the slopes." He checked the heavy black watch on his wrist. "It's late, so I don't think we'll hear anything today, ma'am. Can I do anything else for you?"

Stop calling me "ma'am," she thought. "My name's Riley. What's yours?"

He looked taken aback, but didn't ease his ramrod posture or military-type speech pattern when he said, "Officer Coleman, Todd Coleman."

"Well, Officer Coleman, do you know when Officer Pierce will be coming in?"

"No, ma'am. He's not on any schedule, just filling in, but…" He hesitated, then said, "To be honest, he's in here most nights. I'd think he'll be in tonight."

"Thanks," she said, and he turned and left.

She went back to the cot and tried to work out her emotions. Riley had been so sure she'd know something by now, but it wasn't as bad as it could be. And she had Joshua to thank for that. Despite the casual way he'd announced Charlie wouldn't be in today, she'd been certain he'd talked to Charlie again on her behalf. Obviously their misunderstanding about what she'd been offering him to help her had blown over. That was a relief.

Maybe he'd be back tonight, she thought. Or maybe

he'd be at home. This place wasn't his life. He had a real life with his wife. She dropped down on the cot, then scooted back to rest against the cold stone wall. Some people in this world had love, but she pushed that thought aside. All she asked for in this life was to make it, and to get to that job in San Diego. That wasn't so much to ask for, she thought. It wasn't as though she was asking for happily-ever-after. She sighed, then started counting the stones to pass the time.

IT WAS AFTER ELEVEN o'clock when Joshua entered the station. Vacationing kids at the lifts were wearing out the deputies and taking up a lot of man-hours. Charlie was trying not to make arrests, but if the kids kept up their antics, he'd have no choice when it came to a couple of the worst offenders. For now, things were quiet enough, and with any luck things would stay quiet.

Joshua had left the ranch after J.J. was in bed and asleep, and he'd promised Gen that he'd spend tomorrow with her, his dad and J.J. Gen had told him this morning that he needed to spend more time with his family, right after she'd told him that the prisoner's living conditions had to change. He'd agreed to both.

But he couldn't change the fact that he had to work tonight. That had been part of the bargain he'd made with Charlie. Charlie could go and play Santa during the day, as long as Joshua took the night shift so they had four men on duty all night. Two could do rounds, one could hold down the station, and he'd be there as backup when necessary.

Todd was at a desk near the dispatch radio going over some files, and he looked up as Joshua strode in the side door and headed for his dad's office. "How is everything out there?" Todd called after him.

"According to Charlie, everything's secure for now," he said, and nodded toward the open door to the cell area. "How's everything in here?"

"Quiet." Joshua went into the office and Todd followed him inside. "So you talked to Charlie?"

He'd taken a call from Charlie on the way into the station, a quick exchange of information and a final, "I'll be in to talk to you." He didn't know what Charlie wanted to talk about, but he had a feeling it had to do with Riley. "He just filled me in on the trouble at the lifts."

"He's got a game plan," Todd said. "I hope it works."

Joshua knew that if it were up to Todd, the kids would have been locked up. A by-the-book cop, Charlie had a soft spot when it came to certain types of "criminals." Which was probably why he had let the booking of Riley go the way he had. "Anything come in from Chicago?" he asked as he went around to sit behind his desk.

"Nothing. I think Wes called a Detective Gagne, but he didn't return the call."

Joshua was afraid of that. He didn't want to have to tell Riley. "Does she know?" he asked.

"Yes, she knows," he said as he stood on the other side of the desk, his hands behind his back, his posture rigid.

"Relax, Todd," Joshua said. "Who's on with me tonight?"

He named two backup deputies who would drive the rounds, and then said Wes would pull a double shift. That meant Wes would sleep at the station and Joshua would take care of things unless there was an emergency. "Okay." He glanced at the wall clock. "Time for you to leave, isn't it?"

"I can stay longer, if you need me."

"No," Joshua said, sitting back in the chair and clasping his hands behind his head. "Go home. Everything's under control."

Todd hesitated. "Miss Gen called in earlier, around six, said to tell you to call the house when you got here. She sounded a bit upset."

He'd left the ranch and dropped by the station earlier, before he'd taken a long ride. Gen had probably been annoyed he wasn't home and assumed that he'd be here working. "Thanks, but I've talked to her."

"Oh, good," he said with a touch of relief in his voice. Even Todd didn't like going up against Gen when she was upset.

As Todd left, Joshua looked down at the papers on his desk. Then he checked his voice mail. Nothing. He checked the call box for the station. Only local phone numbers were registered in the log. Three calls came from the same number—his father's ranch—within five minutes of each other. Todd hadn't said Gen had called three times. He logged on to the computer, checked his e-mail, then logged off. Nothing.

Wes looked in, talked for a while, then went off to do some filing. Joshua went out to get some coffee, but stopped when he glanced in the direction of the open security door. Riley was there, standing at the bars, watching him. God, she looked out of place. He steeled himself and headed across the room, stepped through the open door and said, "Hi, there."

"I want you to know I appreciate you keeping the sheriff away from the station today."

She was holding the bars of the cell and staring at him between two of them. "I didn't do anything, except tell him that he did a great Santa impersonation and that he should offer his services to the pageant."

He saw her hands tighten on the bars. "Officer Todd told me that they haven't found out anything today. Is that true?"

He nodded and her head bowed. He could see the soft tendrils of hair that had escaped the confines of the ponytail and the vulnerable line of her neck. "It's true."

She quickly turned away and he had a vision of her doing her screaming therapy. She did utter a low expletive, then exhaled on a harsh rush before she turned back to him. "Now what?"

"We wait," he said. "I've made some calls and as soon as I hear anything—"

"I'll be the first one you tell?"

"Absolutely."

"Well, you know where to find me," she said, not bothering to hide the sarcasm in her tone.

"Do you need food or anything?"

"No, your drill sergeant fed me," she said.

He didn't take offense at her jab, because "drill sergeant" fit Todd Coleman perfectly. He'd always thought the guy had wanted to be a general in the army, but had settled for becoming a police officer. "I hope he was polite."

"He sure was. He did everything but salute."

"Give him time," he murmured, and thought he might have seen a shadow of a smile flit across her face before she killed it. "So how are you feeling now, any dizziness or sickness?"

"I'm not going to faint or throw up."

He wanted to talk more to her, but he felt tongue-tied all of a sudden. What could he say? *Sorry you're locked up? Sorry I can't let you go?* "Good, good," he murmured.

She turned from him to head for the cot. But she didn't lie down. Instead she grabbed an armload of blankets and pillows, then tossed them in the front corner of the cell where he'd found her before. She sank onto the pile with a sigh.

"Why do you keep doing that?" he asked as he watched her sit cross-legged, with her back to the bars and reach for one of the pillows to hug it to her chest.

She turned to look up at him, her blue eyes shaded by the low light and her lashes. "Do what?"

"Sit on the cold floor when you could be on the cot?"

"I like it, and it makes sleeping in my clothes easier."

He hadn't even thought about that. "Do you want me to work out something so you can…sleep comfortably?"

She shook her head and leaned back against the bars. "No, I'm used to it."

"Then use the cot."

"I do, but if I sit here it doesn't seem so…confined."

"What is it, claustrophobia?"

"More like jail-aphobia," she said on a sigh, resting her head against the bars. "Tell me, what's it like outside now?"

"Cold, very cold, and it snowed last night."

"A lot of snow?"

"Ten inches. It took them forever to get the roads cleared."

"I hated the snow when I was growing up. That and the winter wind off the lake." She shivered and he didn't know if she did it on purpose or if it was a spontaneous action. "And the snow got so dirty so fast from all the traffic. All slushy and terrible. I bet it always looks magical around here."

"It stays white for a very long time on the mountains," he said. "At least until the skiers get on it and cut trails."

"Country life," she murmured. "I bet you have a picket fence around your house and holly on your door."

"No, split rail and cattle fencing, and some sort of dried twig thing on the door."

"Oh, I can see it now. A sprawling ranch tucked in the hills, with tons of cows and horses and old-fashioned campfire sing-alongs while you toast marshmallows."

He chuckled softly and she cast him a sideways glance. "We have cattle, not cows, and we have a ranch where you work from morning until night. The only campfires I've been around are the ones when I was in the Boy Scouts."

She closed her eyes again. "Figures," she murmured.

"What figures?"

"For all your talk about being a truant, you were a Boy Scout and went on to be a cop," she said. "I bet you even walk around town now waving to people, getting free cups of coffee from the grateful citizens and stopping by the barbershop to catch up on the latest gossip."

He chuckled. "I wave, I get coffee and I've been known to go to the barbershop from time to time and listen."

This time she glanced at him and he was almost certain she was on the verge of smiling, that the expression teased in the depths of her eyes and at the corners of her mouth. "So, Mr. Policeman Slash Rancher Slash Boy Scout, how does this town smell on a snowy winter's night?"

He wasn't expecting that question. "How does it smell?"

"Smell, as in having an aroma or scent or odor."

"You're a walking thesaurus, aren't you?"

"Just clarifying my question," she murmured.

"Okay, it smells like cold, snow, wood smoke, sometimes there's a trace of coffee or baking in the air, depending on the time of day or night you're inhaling. You know how a small town is?"

"No, I don't know," she said softly without a trace of a smile in her face as she settled against the bars again and closed her eyes. He had the unsettling feeling that she'd just shut him out. He was a bit startled when she spoke in a low voice. "Chicago isn't a small town. It has the cold, but everything else is sort of a mix of traffic and people."

He moved closer to where she sat and crouched on his side of the cell. When he spoke, she seemed slightly startled by his voice, but she didn't open her eyes or turn to him. "What's so important about how the town smells?"

"I just wondered," she said with a touch of wistfulness as she hugged the pillow more tightly to her.

"Joshua?"

He turned to see Wes at the security door. "What's up?"

"Charlie wanted to know if you'd do a foot patrol down toward the bars? A couple of owners asked that since it's Friday, would we keep an eye out for their property."

"No problem. I'll head out in a couple of minutes."

"Thanks," Wes said, then left.

He turned and Riley had twisted around and was looking at him. "Off to do your duty?" she asked. He stood, putting distance between them, then did something he hadn't even considered doing until she'd smiled slightly and said, "Enjoy the snow and the wood smoke and…" She paused. "Everything."

He heard himself saying, "Do you want to see and smell what Silver Creek is like at night after a heavy snow?"

She twisted farther around and looked up at him with those deep blue eyes. "What are you talking about?"

He met her gaze and acted in the most irrational way he had for as long as he could remember. "You heard Wes. I need to walk around the older section of town and check on things. Do you want to get out of

here for a little bit?" It was crazy. He was crazy. But
he didn't take it back. The idea of walking through the
snowy night streets with her was very appealing. He
didn't stop to analyze any of it. "How about it?"

She was on her feet so quickly he barely had time
to absorb the fact that she was up and facing him,
gripping the bars with both hands again and looking
at him wide-eyed, almost wary. "Do you mean it?"

"Yes."

She exhaled on a rush. "Oh, boy, I'd love to."

He turned to enter the security code, but before he
could turn back to pull the door open, she'd tugged it
back and was hurrying over to face him. "Ready to
go?"

He eyed her up and down, the certainty of what he
was doing fading in the wake of why he was doing it.
The obvious answer was the way she looked in her
jeans, the sweatshirt clinging to her high breasts and
the glow of anticipation on her face. He should have
never made the offer. "It's cold out there."

"I'm used to the cold. I'm from Chicago, for Pete's
sake."

He glanced at her bare feet. "They wear boots in
Chicago, don't they? And jackets?"

"Oh, yes, sure," she said. "Just a minute."

She went back into the cell and quickly pulled her
boots out of her duffel bag, then turned to go back with
her light jacket in hand. "I've got this, but my heavy
jacket's in the car." She looked up at him. "You didn't
bring it, did you?"

He shook his head. "No. I didn't." God, he felt like
the Grinch having to tell her there was no Christmas.

"You can't go out there in that jacket." He flicked the cotton with his finger. "It's not made for this weather."

She shook her head. "I'll just get more sweaters and I'll be fine," she said as she turned to reenter the cell.

She wasn't about to let go of this chance, and he found himself making a crazy offer as she crouched over her duffel bag. "I've got a jacket in the office." Before he finished the statement, she was moving toward him.

"Great, great," she said, and kept going, right past him and out the security door.

He found himself playing catch-up as he hurried after her, following her across the squad room and past a surprised Wes. "Joshua, what are—"

He held up a hand and said, "Later," then caught up with Riley just inside the office door.

"Where's the jacket?" she asked, facing him.

He crossed to the rack on the other side of the door and pulled off an extra jacket that he normally left there. Denim, fur-trimmed and at least three sizes too big for her. He turned and held it out. "It'll be too big, but it's definitely warm."

She took it from him and while she put it on, he strapped on a side holster with his father's gun, attached handcuffs and mace to the leather strap of the holster, then turned and laughed when he saw Riley in the jacket. It *was* huge on her. The sleeves barely exposed the tips of her fingers and the shoulder seams looked as if they fell partway down her upper arms. He crossed to get his own jacket and grabbed his hat. "I just need to talk to Wes, then we can leave."

"Terrific," she said, and headed out of his office.

He followed, wondering if he'd ever get a chance to lead, and caught up to her at the desk where Wes was saying, "About fifteen degrees, last I looked."

"It's going to be really cold," she said to Joshua.

"I'm going to do the patrol," Joshua said, addressing Wes. "Got the radio?"

After Wes handed it over, Joshua clipped it to his coat. All the while, Riley stood there, bouncing slightly as she waited. Wes never asked about her and Joshua decided not to say anything about taking her. "I'll be gone an hour. I'll head north."

"Sure," Wes said, then finally let him know he wasn't just going to let the whole Riley thing go unchecked. "Got everything secured?"

Joshua knew what he meant. "Absolutely," he said, then lead the way to the front entrance. But at the double doors, he stopped and took out the handcuffs. She turned, saw the cuffs, then looked up at him, grimacing as if he was holding a snake. "Okay," was all she said as she held out both hands toward him. "Right or left?"

"Right," he said, and she tugged the right jacket sleeve up.

He was struck by how delicate her naked wrist looked as he snapped the cuff on her, then put the other cuff on his left wrist. The phone rang and he looked back as Wes answered it. He waited, then asked, "A problem?"

"Farley at the Grange says he's had trouble with kids after-hours and wanted us to include him on patrol."

"I'll take a look," he said.

Joshua turned to reach for the door and jerked Riley's hand with the motion. "Sorry," he said, pulling back. "I'll try to warn you before I move my hand next time." He tried again, being careful to reach for the door with his right hand. He let Riley slip out in front of him, into the bitterly cold night. He felt her tremble at the contact with the night air and looked down at her as they stood on the top step of the entry. No hat. "Put your collar up," he said.

He lifted his hand so she could raise hers and flip the jacket collar up. "That's better," she said, nestling her chin low.

"Okay, let's go," he said, and moved with her down the two steps and headed toward the main street. They were walking into a cold north wind that came up after dark, swooping down from the higher ranges. It might be fifteen degrees now, but with the windchill factor, it had to be near zero. He wasn't used to it anymore, not after years in Atlanta, and he ducked his head to avoid as much of the breeze as he could. As they approached the corner, he started to push his hands into his pockets, but tangled with Riley again.

He stopped and looked down at her. The dimness of the streetlights barely touched her features. Their hands had to be their pockets in this cold, and he'd forgotten his gloves. "I guess this wasn't such a good idea," he admitted. "I don't have any gloves, and you'll freeze if you can't put your hands in your pockets."

"I don't care about the cold," she said. But he did.

With no other choice, he reached for her hand and put it into his left pocket.

Now, with her fingers curled around his, Riley was

closer to him than she'd ever been. As they walked he could feel her hold on him, her slender fingers entwined with his. Things suddenly got a whole lot more complicated. He realized that he'd been desperate to touch her before, and right now he never wanted to let go.

Chapter Seven

As they walked through town, Riley lengthened her stride to keep up with Joshua.

They walked in silence and she took in everything. The twinkling Christmas lights in the small businesses that lined both sides of the street. Christmas music drifted on the night from a distance and occasionally she could hear laughter. A few cars drove past, most going north, and snow was everywhere, piled on the sides of the street, blocking several parked cars and covering every roof she could see.

All the while, she held on to Joshua's hand, his body heat filtering into hers, and she had a hard time concentrating on the town around them. "This is like something out of a storybook," she said softly.

"So, what does it smell like?" he asked, not looking at her and not breaking stride as they walked along a partially cleared wooden boardwalk that fronted the closed businesses.

She inhaled. "Snow, cold, wood smoke and…" She tested the air again. "Something else, but I'm not sure what." Then she knew. It wasn't from the town, but from the jacket she was wearing. A subtle scent, maybe faint aftershave or soap, most likely from Joshua.

"Maybe it's the Yuppie scent," he said without glancing at her. "They've invaded this place like locusts."

No, it had nothing to do with Yuppies, but she agreed anyway. "Maybe so," she said, and looked straight ahead of them. She couldn't believe that she was walking down a midnight street, not only handcuffed to a cop, but holding his hand, feeling his body heat, recognizing his scent caught in his jacket and actually enjoying it, despite everything, including the fact that he was married. Her fingers could feel the ring, smooth and thin on his finger.

"Have you ever been to Chicago?" she asked for something to say.

"A few times."

"In the winter, there's what I call Chicago snow. It's hard and driving, and it's dirty almost before it hits the ground." She spotted a group of people laughing a couple of blocks away.

"You were born in Chicago?"

"Yeah, and glad to leave it behind. At least, until this all happened."

"There wasn't anything there you didn't want to leave?"

"Nothing."

"What about family?"

"Nothing," she repeated, the word echoing with a certain sadness that she hadn't intended. She never felt sorry for herself and it made her uncomfortable to hear it in her voice. "It was time to move on."

"To San Diego?"

She sighed. "That was the plan. At first I was going to fly, then I spotted that ad and it seemed like a perfect setup. I've never been more wrong in my life."

She felt his eyes on her then, but she didn't meet his gaze. She kept watching a group.

"You were going to San Diego, or you heard about the car, then agreed to go to San Diego?"

"I was going there in the first place for a job."

"Doing what?"

"Not hot-wiring cars, if that's what you're getting at."

He laughed slightly, and she liked the sound. "Then what?"

"Physical therapy."

"How did you get a job in San Diego?"

"Recruiters. One met with me in Chicago, and the job offer came two weeks later." She shivered slightly when the wind gusted in her face. "I just hope I'll still have a job when this gets straightened out."

"Well, sometimes a shortcut or an easy way out of things doesn't work."

She stopped abruptly, forcing him to stop, too, and the motion tugged her hand out of his pocket and into air that was even colder when he let go of her. His eyes were shadowed by the night and his hat, but she didn't miss the tightness at his mouth and jaw. "I'm tired of all of this," she said. "Let me say this as clearly as possible. I answered the ad, and the attorney checked on me, then hired me, and that's it. It wasn't some shortcut." She hesitated. "Okay, it was, sort of, but not the way you mean it. It meant I could cash in my plane ticket and have more money for when I got to San Diego, and drive a nice car on the trip."

"If a company recruited you, they paid for your relocation, didn't they?"

"Of course they did, but I didn't have anything else to live on until I got settled." She exhaled and her warm breath curled into the frigid air between them. "Do you know what it is like to barely have enough money to live, and not a penny more?"

"Of course I do," he said without hesitating.

"You said that too quickly. It sounds as if you've had family all your life, and you've had backing, and you've had a great job in Atlanta." She shook her head softly and that echo of loneliness was there again. God, she hated it.

Oddly, his reaction wasn't what she expected. "No one knows what a person goes through," he said in a low voice.

"No," she murmured, and started walking again.

He was beside her, matching his stride to hers now, and when his hand caught hers and tugged it back into his pocket, she tried not to feel the touch of his cold wedding band when it pressed against her finger. She just held to him and kept going. It didn't make sense that she only wanted to keep holding on to him and to ask him what he'd been through, why he hated the nights like she did, why he'd know what it was like to be alone.

She glanced at him, but he was staring straight ahead at the group that was only half a block away now and laughing uproariously. "Are these people the ones you've come out to look for?"

"No, they're having a good time," he said, and they were right by them. Joshua pulled her closer to the edge of the walkway to let the people pass, murmured, "Good evening," and then they went on their way.

Joshua started off again, slower this time, and she looked ahead, noticing a slight glow in the night sky off in the distance. "What's that light?" she asked.

"Ski runs at the inn. The public lifts are closed at midnight, but the inn has twenty-four-hour skiing if the guests want it. One of their perks. Anything you want. Anything money can buy. Night skiing is simple compared to some of the luxuries people want."

"You've been there?"

"Jack Prescott, the owner, grew up here, and we've been friends for years."

"Rich friends in high places?"

"Old friends," he murmured. "Jack's great-great-grandfather founded this town. Set up his silver stake, almost died doing it, then pulled off with one of the biggest strikes in the area. He named it Silver Creek, built the first buildings, and the rest is history."

"So Jack was born with a silver spoon in his mouth?"

"Sure, but he's smart and a hard worker. He's made things happen that others just dreamed about. He's like the old man, making things happen."

"You don't do this very often, do you?" she asked, slightly breathless in the biting cold.

"Do what?"

"Take prisoners with you on a nightly walk?"

"No," he said.

"Why did you do it?" she asked.

Her question made him stop walking, then he looked down at her. She didn't expect him to say, "I don't know." But he did, then he started walking again.

This time she skipped to keep up and finally tugged on him, but kept her hand in his pocket. "Can we go slower?" He slowed the pace to a comfortable stroll. "Thanks. Your wife must have to go into training to keep up with you."

He didn't stop, but said, "My wife's dead." He didn't break stride or look at her. He kept moving, and, for a moment, she thought she had to have misheard him. Or imagined what she'd thought he said.

"Excuse me?" she asked, watching him as they kept walking.

"She's dead. Gone. Passed away." Then she felt his hand tighten on hers, just a bit, but noticeably. "What is it they say, 'I lost her'? But that means you can find someone again. Stupid expression," he muttered, and tucked his chin lower in his collar.

She was literally at a loss for words. All this time she'd assumed a wife was at home waiting for him. She'd even thought Gen had been his wife at first. But his wife was dead. That caught her off guard. She felt an overwhelming sadness for the man beside her. A sense that deepened when his hand tightened slightly on hers and she felt the wedding band press into her skin.

Everything made sense to her now. Him leaving his job in Atlanta, coming back here, working all night. And no wonder he hated the nights and knew what it was to be lonely. The sadness formed an ache deep inside her, and she realized they'd walked almost a full block and his words still hung between them. She hadn't said a thing.

"I'm really sorry," she said finally, and knew how inadequate the words were.

He slowed and stopped, then glanced at her, but didn't turn to her. He kept her hand in his pocket, never letting go, and his face was shadowed, so she couldn't read any expression there. "So am I," he said on a rough whisper.

Her ache grew. "I just had no idea. No one said anything about it."

"That surprises me," he murmured. "I thought that's all they did was talk about me, about poor old Joshua. Although they never talk about it to my face anymore. It's as if it never happened."

"That's the worst, isn't it?" she asked, and knew from her own experience how awful it was when people pretended that a deep loss never happened. "It's like if they don't talk about it, it won't hurt, or you'll just move past it?"

He exhaled and his warm breath curled into the frigid air, disappearing into the night around them. "You do understand," he said. A statement, not a question. "You're the only one who's ever said that. Not even my father."

She understood. She knew what it was to have people shut off everything. Don't talk to the orphan about her parents. Don't stir up her painful memories. She hated it then and she hated it now.

Joshua turned slightly toward Riley, stunned by what he'd just told her. And more stunned that he had said the words without bracing himself, without making sure he'd survive saying them out loud. Before, he'd wanted to talk, but when the others ignored it, he took that as a gift. But as he spoke to Riley, he knew that the gift hadn't been for him, but for them.

His dad and Gen couldn't say the words anymore. It was as if knowing they couldn't help him, they chose to avoid it altogether. Now he was talking to Riley and feeling as if the words he'd said had settled something. He just wasn't sure what it was.

"It's hard on everyone," she said, and shivered.

He didn't think before reaching out with his free hand and touching her cold cheek with the tips of his fingers. The connection was barely there, but it felt oddly as if it anchored him, the way her hand in his was becoming an anchor. "You're cold," he said. He wasn't sure why, but an uneasiness was growing in him. "We should head back to the station."

"No, not yet," she said quickly as her grip tightened.

The fear grew, a strange fear that had no name, but was lingering on the fringes of his feelings. He took a deep breath, letting the frigid air into his lungs. It was a strange night and got even stranger when he agreed to her request. "Okay, a bit farther." And he turned from her and continued walking.

He was overly conscious of her hand in his, her closeness as they walked, and she didn't say anything for a very long time. She startled him when she finally spoke. "So what do you do on foot patrol?"

They were passing the old hotel, heading north. "Walk and look," he said, and realized he had to finish something that was bothering him. "How did you know about that?"

She didn't ask for a clarification. She knew what he was asking. "My parents were killed, and it was suddenly as if they'd never existed. I know people wanted to spare me more pain, and they thought if they brought up the subject it would hurt me. They were wrong."

"Sarah died eighteen months ago," he heard himself saying, and couldn't give details. His throat tightened just saying her name. "At the year mark everyone seemed to decide that was it, that it was time to move on. A year allowed for mourning, then you're done."

She sighed heavily and thankfully didn't ask to hear more. "People like rules, I guess. Life goes on. Time heals all wounds. Rules. Platitudes."

She knew. She understood, and there was an easing in Joshua. A sense of freedom that he hadn't felt for what seemed forever. And it was because of her. He didn't dare look at Riley right then, because he wasn't sure what he'd do. Instead he kept walking, kept looking ahead of them, and holding on to her hand.

Riley didn't want to look at Joshua. Eighteen months and he still wore his wedding ring. He was still hurting. She could feel it in him, hear it in every word he spoke, in the way he held to her hand. She was little more than a stranger to him, but she felt as if she'd glimpsed the man's soul. She envied a woman who could pull that much love out of a man, and she found that she didn't want to talk about the sadness anymore. "So what are we looking for on this foot patrol?" she made herself ask.

"Anything out of place, or anyone who looks suspicious."

All she saw was snow and the peacefulness of a winter's night. The town was postcard-pretty and she could barely imagine why they needed a police force. Then she saw a shadow at the next street. It was a man. He stepped into the light of the nearest store windows. Even from the distance of a good half block, Riley knew he was drunk. He was keeping himself steady by keeping one hand on the buildings. He walked toward Riley and Joshua and she could hear him muttering, maybe singing.

"Now, he looks suspicious," she whispered as she moved closer to Joshua.

"Sure does," he said in a low voice. Then, "Let's go check him out."

The closer they got, the drunker the man looked. Joshua stopped a few feet from the man and said, "Pudge? What's going on?"

Joshua knew him? His name was Pudge? Even in his heavy outdoor clothes, the man looked hawkishly thin. At the sound of his name, Pudge stopped, still holding on to the wall for support. He wore a fur jacket and a matching hat that was so askew his left earflap was almost covering his left eye, pirate-style. "Hey, Joshua." His breath smelled one-hundred proof.

"What are you doing out here this time of night?" Joshua asked. "Isn't your bar open?"

He waved his free hand and almost hit Joshua on the arm. "The bar's in good hands...Linus...said he can do it. So, old Pudge took off. Got trouble, and left."

"What trouble?"

Pudge coughed and shook his head slowly. "Real trouble, Josh, real trouble," he muttered thickly, and leaned closer to the two of them. "Woman trouble," he huffed and almost fell into them. He caught himself with one hand on Joshua's chest and pushed himself back, grabbing for the wall again. "You people," he muttered in Riley's direction. "You're nothing but trouble. Oh, you're pretty enough, cute, sexy, hot, but real trouble." He straightened a bit with his hand still on the wall. "Now, I gotta go. Gotta get to…" He frowned. "Oh, Annie's. Yeah, gotta get to Annie's."

"You need help getting there?" Joshua asked.

"Thash…thash….am I going south?" he asked, pointing down the street.

"Looks that way."

"More snow tonight?"

"Not for a while."

"I can make it," he mumbled thickly, and lurched past them.

Riley turned to watch as Pudge headed south, then she glanced at Joshua. "Is that small-town policing, to let a drunk just go like that?"

He shrugged, then turned and started for the corner, making her skip to catch up. "He's got enough trouble with that wife of his. And he's going just down the block to Annie's, at the hotel." He turned the corner Pudge had appeared at and they were on a quiet side street. "He'll sleep it off, but I think I need to take a walk past his bar," he said, pointing down the street with his free hand. "There it is."

She saw the only open place on the street; an old stone building with tall, narrow windows, each lit up by a neon beer sign. The Briar. "You're going to his bar?"

He kept walking. "Yeah. I'll take a look and see who this Linus is, and make sure he isn't stealing Pudge blind."

She stopped, forcing him to do the same. He looked down at her. "What's wrong?"

"What'll you say when they ask who I am and why I'm with you?"

He stared at her long and hard, then unexpectedly touched her cheek again, but this time the warmth of his fingertips lingered on her cold skin. She couldn't stop trembling and covered it with a fake shiver as if she was affected by the bitter cold and not by the man's touch.

"I'll tell them you're trouble and that I have to keep an eye on you."

Joshua meant it. Riley was trouble, and it wasn't because of the stolen car. He'd told her about Sarah. He'd found out she'd had her share of pain in life. He'd realized that it had been easier talking to her than with anyone else in a very long time. He was holding her hand and hadn't thought about letting it go.

And to make matters even more confusing, he was staring at her softly parted lips and knew she was trouble with a capital "T" because he wanted nothing more than to kiss her.

Instead he pulled away, breaking the contact of his fingers on her skin and pushed his hand back in his pocket. Trouble. His trouble, not hers.

"It's up to you about how you introduce me." She tugged their hands out of his pocket and held them up. "But how are you going to explain this?"

"Keep your hand in my pocket and they'll never have to know," he said.

"Won't they think it's strange that I'm walking around with my hand in your pocket?"

Realizing this could get tricky, Joshua undid his jacket and withdrew the keys. He unlocked the cuffs.

Once they were separated, he said, "Just stay close, and let me do all the talking. Okay?"

She nodded. "You got it."

She stayed right by his side, so close in fact that her arm bumped against his when they stepped up onto the cleared walkway at the door to the bar. The Briar had been here for as long as he could remember, first run by Pudge's uncle, then by Pudge. The building was shrouded in snow, but the path to the entry was completely cleared.

He reached for the door and allowed Riley to enter first. He followed her into warmth, the music and laughter, and the heady mixture of wood smoke that came from the massive stone fireplace. Riley stopped and motioned toward the bar. "Is that him, this Linus person?"

Joshua looked over in that direction and saw a stranger behind the bar. The guy was laughing uproariously at something a blonde sitting at the bar had said. Joshua watched him for a moment, assessing him. The guy could be approaching fifty, but he dressed like someone's idea of a lounge lizard in a Vegas casino. His shirt was black silk, unbuttoned almost to his navel, worn with black leather pants that looked maybe a size too small. His patently dyed dark hair was spiked the way a teenager would wear it, and he looked a little drunk.

"Let's go see," he said, and they made their way to

the bar. Joshua slipped onto a stool at the nearest end of the bar, and Riley sat next to him. He glanced at the smoky mirrors set behind the glass shelves that held what looked like an unlimited supply of liquor and saw Riley in the reflection. She'd pushed her collar down and unbuttoned his jacket as she watched the man behind the bar. Then she turned and met Joshua's gaze in the mirror.

Joshua looked away and called, "Hey, there."

The man walked a bit unsteadily over to them. "What'll it be for you two gorgeous people?" he asked, and actually winked at Riley.

"Where's Pudge?" Joshua asked, barely getting any of the man's attention.

"Gone," the guy said, then actually looked at Joshua. Realization dawned on the man despite his being drunk, his eyes widening, then darting to Riley and back to Joshua again. He dropped a towel he'd been holding and held out both hands palms out. "Hey, he had to go….said he had to…and I…I was just helping him."

"I think it's closing time," Joshua said.

The guy looked ready to argue, then the woman he'd been talking to, a brassy blonde who Joshua hadn't seen before, waved a napkin at him. "Hey, lover, here's my number."

"Catch you later," Linus said quickly, and reached under the bar. He came out with a leather jacket he quickly put on, then headed for the blonde. "Hey, honey bunny, how about you and me go down the way where there's real nightlife?"

She went with him toward the door. "It's a date, lover boy."

Before Joshua was off the stool, Linus and his blonde were out the door. Joshua looked over the room at the ten or so people who remained. "Closing time," he announced, and within five minutes, the room was empty.

"Well, talk about clearing the house," Riley murmured as she spun around on her stool.

"It's a talent," he said. "Pudge can clean up tomorrow when he sobers up. We'll just go to the door, flip off the lights and make sure the lock's on when we leave. Let's check the back door."

"I'll do it," she said quickly, and left the room. But the moment she was out of sight, Joshua heard the sound of a door closing with a sharp thud. Kicking himself for being such a fool, he ran after her.

Chapter Eight

Joshua sprinted after Riley, turned the corner and ran right into her as she came back. The impact knocked her into the wall that held two pay phones and he grabbed her by the shoulders of his jacket. "Damn," he muttered as she steadied herself.

"What?" she gasped, looking up at him with huge eyes. Then she started to laugh. She was really laughing, not chuckling, not tittering, but laughing out loud and starting to bend over, her arms around her middle as if in an ineffective effort to control her humor. The shoulders of the jacket she was wearing shook, and he stepped back half a pace.

"What's so funny?" he asked.

She straightened and sobered a bit, but the smile didn't die, or that amusement in her eyes. "You. That look on your face. You thought I was making a run for it, didn't you?"

He wanted to say he hadn't thought that, but that's exactly what he'd thought. "Did you lock the door?"

"It's locked, Officer, and the prisoner is secured…for now." She held out her hands to him, palms up. "Maybe you should put the cuffs back on me?"

He ignored her words and turned away from her, hating the way his heart was still beating too fast and the way she could bring a life to him that he'd almost forgotten existed. "We're leaving," he said, and headed toward the entry. She was right behind him as he locked up. "Put up your collar. It's cold out there."

She did as he said, flipped up the big collar, then tucked her chin into the front of the jacket. "Ready," she said, and he let her exit first, then he followed her and pulled the door securely shut. It was starting to snow again, a light flurry in the night, and he pushed both his hands into his pockets, hunching into the wind. Silently they walked together down to the end of the street, then headed back in the direction of the station.

When they got to the Old Silver Creek Hotel, he didn't see Pudge anywhere, and hoped he was inside sleeping it off. He looked into the lobby, but it was barely lit and no one was in sight.

"Do you think he made it?" Riley asked.

"I hope so."

"If you want to check, feel free. I don't have anything else to do," she said. "Go on in and I'll wait here for you."

As silly as it sounded, he believed she probably would wait, but he didn't take her up on it.

"We'll both go in and check," he said, touching her arm to get her to go with him. "The last thing I want is Pudge passed out in the snow somewhere."

They entered the quiet lobby. The place hadn't

changed since Annie and her husband had taken it over years ago. Dark mahogany, polished and well taken care of, was everywhere. Fresh flowers, even in the dead of winter, brightened up the room, and Annie's Christmas tree, decorated with tinsel and gold ornaments, stood in the main window of the lobby. The tree had been a fixture every Christmas since they'd reopened the hotel.

Annie came out of the back room and grinned at him. "Hey, Joshua," she said, then saw Riley. Her grin didn't falter. "Hello, there."

"Just checking to see if Pudge made it here okay?"

"Yeah, he's sleeping it off in the attic room. Poor guy, that wife of his can be harsh."

"I just wanted to make sure he hadn't passed out somewhere between here and the Briar. When he comes around in the morning, tell him I locked up for him?"

"Sure thing. Rick was wondering if he should run down and do it, but since you've taken care of it, that makes life simpler."

She glanced at Riley again. "Aren't you going to introduce me?" she asked.

"Annie, this is Riley Shaw, and Riley, this is Annie Logan. She owns this place."

Annie came around the desk and held out both hands to Riley. How she managed to find Riley's hands in the long cuffs, Joshua didn't know, but the two women were smiling at each other as they clasped hands, and he sensed Annie knew exactly who Riley was. She knew everything that happened in Silver Creek. "So how do you like our little town?"

"It's lovely," Riley said, stepping back to look around the lobby. "And this is really nice."

"Thanks," Annie said, then looked at Joshua. "I'll give Pudge your message."

He nodded, then touched Riley on the arm. "Let's go." They headed back out into the night and as they walked, the snow started coming down hard.

He hesitated once they reached the station and looked down at Riley in the glow of the light over the entrance. Snow fell all around her and her hair was touched by the glimmering whiteness. Before he could say anything, she held out her right hand. "You'd better put the handcuffs back on," she said.

She was right. He didn't want to explain to Wes why he'd been wandering around in the dead of night with a prisoner who wasn't restrained. He reached for the handcuffs, then reluctantly snapped one on her wrist, before putting the other one on him. He looked into her upturned face and did something that made no sense. He apologized to her. "I'm sorry for having to do that."

"Me, too," she whispered.

He hesitated, then turned and went with her up the steps and into the station. Wes was at the front desk watching TV. He looked over at them. "How did things go?"

"I locked up for Pudge at the bar," he said, going around the desk with Riley. He stopped and took the cuff off Riley's wrist, then his own. As Riley shrugged out of his jacket, he spoke to Wes. "Can you take Miss Shaw back to her cell?"

"Sure thing," Wes said as he came over to them.

Riley handed him the jacket and said, "Thanks for the loan."

"No problem."

"Joshua, you had a message come in. Some guy named Harvey Sills. He said he's been pulling a long night and he wanted to talk to you, but he'll call back when the shift's over. He didn't say who he was or anything."

"He's a P.I. in Chicago."

Riley's gaze flew to Joshua. "Chicago?"

"He's got connections, and even does some work for the Chicago P.D. I thought he might be able to find out a few things for me."

"Call him," she said, desperation tingeing her voice. She even grabbed his arm. "Please."

He looked at the wall clock. "It's one-thirty here, so in Chicago it's later."

"Just call," she said, her hold on him getting tighter.

If he could get the answers she wanted, he would have done it right then, but he knew he couldn't. "I'll call him back first thing in the morning."

He knew she was upset, but she let go of his arm and, with just a quick glance at him, went quietly toward the lockdown area. Wes followed her. Joshua watched the empty doorway for a moment, heard the cell door being opened and then clanged shut. As Wes automatically reached to pull the security door closed behind him, Joshua said, "Leave that door open" at the same time he heard Riley call, "Please, don't close the door."

Wes glanced back into the cell area, then pushed the door back against the wall. "How's that?" he asked Riley.

"Fine, thanks," Joshua heard her say.

Wes looked at him as he crossed to Joshua. "Is that fine with you, too?"

"Yes, it is," he said. He heard a thud in the cell, then a sound of movement.

"Good," Wes said, then added, "Banks is coming in. He didn't think he'd be back until tomorrow, but he's in town and ready to work. Charlie said if he asked, to tell him to come in and let you off for the night."

Joshua knew Riley had moved something in the cell area, and he also knew he wasn't going to stay. "When's he getting here?"

Wes glanced at the clock. "Five minutes, maybe sooner."

"I'm out of here," he said, and headed for the office. He took off his uniform jacket, put on the jacket that Riley had worn, then turned off the lights and made to leave.

But as he stepped out of the office, he looked toward the security door and even in the dim light, he could see Riley sitting on the floor again, her back to the bars, her head resting on her bent knees. He really had to go. He called to Wes, "Make sure that door stays open, and get her whatever she needs."

"You've got it," Wes said as he sat to watch more TV.

Joshua went out into the biting cold and sat in his Jeep in the security lot for a lot longer than it took for the heater to start working and the seats to warm up. He'd never been a man to fool himself. Maybe that was part of why he was good cop. He looked at things head-on, saw them for what they were and dealt with them.

He flipped on his windshield wipers and as the snow cleared, he could see the side door to the station. But what he really saw was his life for the past few hours. For so long, his life had seemed out of focus, but in the past few hours it seemed to make more sense.

But it was focusing on the wrong things, or the wrong person. Riley Shaw, a suspected car thief, the one person he'd talked to about Sarah. No one else really talked about his wife anymore. Riley was right, it was as if they were pretending she never existed. He exhaled, then put the vehicle in gear and backed out, swinging onto the night street in the heavily falling snow.

Riley Shaw was trouble. That had been the naked truth. But it was his trouble. He'd been alone too long, he reasoned, isolated for a year and a half. He'd been alone, even in a crowd or with family. And tonight, for a brief moment or two, he hadn't felt alone. He'd felt connected in some way that had nothing to do with the handcuffs.

He struck the top of the steering wheel with the flat of his hand. He'd come home, where he'd been as a kid, and now he was reacting like a teenager with out-of-control hormones. One look into blue eyes and all bets were off. There was no way he could have spent the night at the station with Riley there. Going back to the ranch was the smart thing to do. He just wondered why driving away from the station and Riley made him feel so horribly alone.

RILEY WOKE SLOWLY, not sure if she was dreaming about a tiny voice singing an unintelligible song or if there really was someone singing close by. She stirred and slowly opened her eyes. But it was no dream. The cold bars were here, and the gray walls. The voice was still here, too.

The singing stopped. "You be up," the voice said near her ear, and Riley jerked to a sitting position, blinking, twisting in the cot, and couldn't believe her eyes.

In the next cell was a cherub. A blond, blue-eyed, rosy-cheeked cherub staring at her through the heavy bars. The vision clapped her hands together with glee, then darted to the stripped cot, climbed on it and proceeded to bounce up and down, chanting, "Good, good, good!"

Riley rubbed at her eyes while the chanting went on and on, and she knew this wasn't a cherub. Cherubs didn't wear denim overalls or have their hair in twin braids, or wear bandages on their foreheads. "What…. what's going on?" she asked.

The child had the decency to stop bouncing, scramble off the cot and come over to the bars again. She pressed her face against the cold metal and huge blue eyes stared at Riley without blinking. "Who are you?" she asked in a tiny voice.

"Riley," she said. "And who are you?"

"J.J." She reached one hand between the bars and held up three fingers. "I'm free."

"Why are you in jail?"

The tiny girl frowned. "Huh?"

"How did you get here?"

"Mamaw comed."

"Who's Mamaw?"

"That would be me," a voice said, and Riley turned to see Gen enter the cell area and cross to the next cell. "J.J., get out of there right now."

She looked at Gen. "She's Riley."

"I know Riley. And you know you aren't supposed to be in here."

The little girl looked ready to pout, but then did as she was told when Gen opened the cell door. Once the little girl was out, Gen crouched in front of her. "Go and tell Daddy to get the crayons from his desk so you can draw a pretty picture."

J.J. looked back at Riley. "Me got crayons."

"Good for you."

Then the child darted off and out of the cell area. Riley heard her calling, "Daddy! Daddy! Crayons!"

Gen came over to Riley's cell. "Sorry about that, but J.J. moves so fast, it's hard to keep up with her."

Riley sat forward, and brushed her hands over her face. "What's going on?" she asked.

"I came down to make sure you got your shower and to see if you had laundry that needed doing. J.J. had to come along because her papa had to sit with a sick horse."

Riley looked at Gen. "Who is she?" she asked.

"Joshua's daughter, our granddaughter."

Joshua's daughter? All she'd thought about after he'd left last night was the call from Chicago and that moment on the street when he'd said his wife was dead. "She's cute," she said for lack of anything else to say.

"She's a lot like Sarah. Hopefully she'll grow up to be as good and kind as her mother."

Now Joshua's dead wife had a name. Sarah, and had the description of being good and kind. "Hopefully she will be," she murmured as she tugged the band out of her hair and shook it loose.

She didn't ask, but Gen kept going on about Sarah as Riley got to her feet and stretched. "Sarah was wonderful. She was born into one of the wealthiest families in Atlanta, but you'd never know it. She volunteered all the time and helped people, and was a terrific wife and mother."

She sounded like a saint who'd had an angelic child with a man who still mourned her passing. Riley combed her fingers through her tangled hair and didn't bother to figure out why she suddenly felt so depressed. "He said she died."

"He told you about her?" she asked, obviously surprised.

Riley nodded. "Last night he said she'd died."

"That's odd. He never talks about her anymore," Gen said with a slight frown, then glanced at the wall clock. "It's eight o'clock. Are you ready for your shower?"

"Yes, but first I need to talk to Joshua."

"How about a shower first, then—"

"No, I really need to talk to him now. It's important."

"Okay," she said. "I'll get him." And she left.

Riley brushed at her tangled hair as she stood by the cell door and watched Gen cross the squad room to the open door of the office.

When Joshua stepped inside, he looked irritatingly fresh in an open-necked, beige flannel shirt. His hair was slicked back from his face, and he looked as if he'd just shaved. "I was just going to come in and talk to you."

She felt her breath catch. "What did your Chicago connection say?"

"He didn't have anything specific, but he's getting all the information he can on you and the car owner. It should come in soon."

A lot of her anticipation evaporated at his words. Although she thought everything in her juvenile record would be sealed, she wasn't sure. A man who had been married to a saint wouldn't look kindly at the record she'd amassed while she'd been under the jurisdiction of the Juvenile Court.

"More waiting," she said on a sigh.

"I think we've got the weekend to get through," he said. "Things just don't move quickly on weekends, especially on weekends just before big holidays."

"Does that mean you can't book me on the weekend?"

"Of course you can be booked anytime, but there's no point in doing it right now, unless you want to get it over with."

"No, I don't want to get it over with. I mean, I do, but I don't want to make things worse." She shrugged and grimaced. "Then again, how much worse can this get?"

She could see by the look on his face that he knew exactly how much worse it could get. So did she. "Charlie's going to be in later, but he's got practicing to do for the pageant. The torches are tricky."

"Torches for Santa?"

"Yeah, he comes down the ski slope with torches. That's part of the presentation. Then he takes his spot on the throne they build out of snow, and he greets the kids." He tucked the tips of his fingers into the pockets of his jeans. "The question is whether or not he'll insist on the booking, and my guess is, he won't until Monday." He turned to the control panel, hit his codes, and came back to slide her door open. He stood in the entryway to her cell, inches away from her.

"Joshua," someone called from the outer room. "Phone. It's a Detective Gagne from Chicago."

He turned, and she was right beside him, hurrying with him out of the cell area into the squad room. Banks, an officer who'd come in sometime during the night, was at a nearby desk holding out the phone to Joshua. He was thin and sharp-looking, with eyes that narrowed when he saw Riley. "You want to take it here?"

"Sure," Joshua said, and took the phone from him. "Detective Gagne, Officer Pierce here. What do you have for me?"

He listened for what seemed forever, then he said, "Okay. Get back to me." Then hung up.

"What?" she asked, grabbing his arm. She felt his muscles tense under her grip, but she didn't care. She only cared about what he'd just heard on the phone.

"Nothing," he said, glancing at her hand on him. "They can't contact the owner, but his secretary is the one who filed the complaint. She said the car was stolen from his house, and she doesn't know anything else about it."

She felt her legs turn to jelly and she sank into the nearest chair. "The owner? Where's he?"

"She doesn't know. He took off, probably for the holidays. He's been going through a divorce and she said he needed time away and apparently took it."

She leaned forward, burying her head in her hands. This just went from bad to worse. "They tricked me, didn't they?" she muttered.

"I don't know," Joshua said, and she realized that his voice was very close, so close she felt the heat of his breath on the back of her hands. She slowly lowered her hands and he was inches from her, crouched at her eye level. "The car's stolen. You were driving. Give me something, anything, that can change those facts."

Her stomach clenched. "I've told you everything."

His eyes were intense and she could see the flare of amber at the irises. "Listen, if you were set up, they'll find out in Chicago. You'll go back and you'll—"

"I can't go back there," she said, raw fear deep inside her. She didn't want to ever see a police station in Chicago again, or the city itself for that matter.

"You won't have a choice," he said in a low voice.

"But you said I'd have until Monday at least," she noted, hoping against hope that Monday would bring some good news. She didn't know if it would, but she didn't want to leave this place. Even though it was a jail, and this man was her jailer, she felt almost safe here. She felt… She bit her lip hard. No, she couldn't feel anything for anyone around here. If she had to go back, so be it.

"Monday," Joshua said, then touched her hand that was clenched on her thigh. "And until then, use that time to think of anything that can help."

The memory of him holding her hand as they walked down the night streets was so vivid that it was all she could do to jerk back from his contact and away from her own reactions right then. "I will," she whispered.

Joshua pulled his hand back and pressed it to his thigh. He hadn't meant to come in today, but he'd found himself at the station on the pretext of getting some paperwork to work on at the ranch. Now he was here with Riley, watching her, and he was ridiculously close to touching her again. To holding her hand, and to telling her that he'd do what he could to get her out of this. But that wasn't his job, and it wasn't his fight or his right to do anything like that. But one thing he could do was talk Charlie into waiting until Monday. And he would.

"I'll wait for Harvey to call, and Gagne said he'll try some friends of the owner."

"Then what?"

"That's it. Either you're booked, or we'll cut you loose." God, he never should have come back here. "We'll wait and see," was all he could bring himself to say. Then he was saved by J.J. running out of his office and coming over to them.

She went right to him where he hunkered down in front of Riley, caught his face between her two small hands and said, "Daddy promised."

He had promised he was going to let her draw while he got his papers. He looked over at Gen, who was watching the scenario from the next desk. "Can you take care of the shower?" he asked, straightening.

"Sure."

He looked back down at the still-seated Riley. "Get your shower, and I'll make sure you get breakfast."

She stood, just inches from him. "Thank you," she said in a low voice.

Then J.J. pushed between them, one hand on Riley's leg and one hand on his. "Daddy? Hurry," she said.

He looked down at her and scooped her up into his arms, glancing from her to Riley then back at his daughter. J.J. had met Riley and clearly liked her. That made him a little uneasy, and he wasn't ready to analyze why. "Okay," he said, "let's find those crayons."

She held on to him with her arm around his neck and he didn't look back at the two women behind him. He went right into his office and, for the first time in a long time, he closed the door behind him.

Chapter Nine

Joshua settled J.J. at his desk with a cup of crayons and some paper. While she started drawing, he reached for the phone and put in a call to Harvey in Chicago.

He got him on the first ring. "It's Joshua," he said. "Hope I didn't wake you up."

"No chance, but I don't have anything yet."

He told him about his conversation with Detective Gagne and ended with, "And I was thinking, maybe you could concentrate on the owner's private life? The separation and anything else going on?"

"What do you have in mind?" Harvey asked bluntly.

"I don't know, but I think there's an outside possibility that she might have been set up. The logical place to start is the owner."

"An insurance scam?"

"Could be. The car's worth a lot of money. And if he's got financial problems, who knows?"

"Okay, you've got it. Anything else?"

"Just get all you can on everyone involved, including Miss Shaw. I need anything you can get."

He hung up, stared at the phone, then tried Gagne again to ask him if there was any trace of a setup from what he could tell, but the detective didn't answer. He thought of leaving a message, then hung up without saying anything. He'd ask him the next time he called.

He'd barely put the phone back on the cradle when it rang. He answered quickly and was surprised to hear Harvey's voice again. "Hey, what's up?"

"Just got a couple of faxes on my inquiries. Riley Shaw graduated from the local university, good grades, no incidents at all. Seems she worked to subsidize a scholarship."

That didn't fit with a car thief at all, but sure fit with what she'd told him. "Anything else?"

"Not on Shaw, but that attorney you asked me to check on? He's on a fishing boat in the Florida Keys, out of contact, and most likely won't be back until after New Year's."

When Joshua hung up, he looked at J.J. who was bent over the desk, earnestly scribbling on the paper. Joshua left her to her creative process and stepped out of his office. Gen was at the front desk talking to Stella, a part-time secretary who came in on weekends to catch up with the paperwork. The radio crackled with chatter that he didn't bother to follow. Instead, he headed back to the cell area.

There was no one there. But when he turned to go back to J.J., Riley was entering, wearing fresh jeans and an oversize white shirt, her feet bare. Her damp hair fell around her shoulders and her face looked scrubbed. She was beautiful, and she probably didn't even know it. She didn't act like a woman who knew men were looking at her with more then a little interest.

Gen smiled at him. "Josh, we really need to get something done about accommodations for women around here."

"You should listen to Gen. I think this might be illegal to house me like you're housing me."

"I doubt that, but I'm open to any suggestions."

Gen said, "Start by asking for a television." Then with a wave of her hand, she said to Joshua, "See you later. I'll get J.J. and head on back. You get there as soon as you can. Remember, you promised."

That was the second reminder that he'd promised to be home today to spend time with all of them. "Sure thing," he said, standing aside to let Riley through the security door.

He watched her go into the open cell as if she belonged there. But he knew she didn't. Right then, he knew that was a fact. He couldn't prove it. She sure couldn't, but she didn't belong in this jail, in that cell. Or maybe it was wishful thinking that a woman who seemed to be opening up dark places in his soul and letting in the light, couldn't be what the lack of facts said she was. "I'm not sure about a TV, but how about some pink curtains?" he asked, more to hide from his own thoughts than for any other reason.

She turned to look at him. "Oh, sure, and embroidered silk pillows? Personally, I think it's pretty fancy to have a curtain up, hanging from the pipes. Much better than that cardboard screen."

He shrugged. "We don't usually have female prisoners here. No, that's not right. Years ago, Maddy

Sloan was in here a few times. We called her Mad Maddy, and Dad would bring her in when he'd find her driving around town. She never had a license, didn't really know how to drive, but every once in a while she'd go hunting for her husband, and Dad would have to get her here, then get her husband to come in and take her home."

"And what was Mad Maddy's husband's name, Insane Ike?"

He smiled at that, and found he liked smiling with Riley. "Owen Sloan. He was her first husband, and good old Pudge was Maddy's second husband."

"Oh, now that's interesting," she murmured as she sank onto the cot and brushed her damp hair back from her makeup-free face. "Very interesting."

He stood in the open cell door and leaned one shoulder against the metal frame, not about to move closer. "Even more interesting is the fact that Pudge's second wife was Owen Sloan's sister."

Her pale lips curved softly in a smile. "If you tell me his third wife was Owen Sloan's mother, I'll probably be sick again."

"No, he got his third wife off a chorus line in Vegas. Lasted a year with her, and she was gone."

"Wife number four?"

"Wife number four, the current Mrs. Pudge, is Williamette Smith, and she was the widow of the minister who used to preach at the local church. Pastor Smith died and she married Pudge exactly one year later. Can't figure out why, because they mix like oil and water."

She chuckled at that and the sound ran riot over his

nerves. "So she marries a bartender who drinks too much and who has had three other wives?"

"I guess she thought she could reform him."

"Well, good luck to her," she said as she pulled her legs up to sit cross-legged on the cot. "He doesn't look reformed, and he doesn't look like a man named Pudge, either."

He crossed his arms on his chest, not at all anxious to leave, even though he'd promised Gen he'd get back to the ranch soon. "Now that's an interesting story, too. Seems when he was a kid, he was…well, overly fond of food. He was pretty big, from what Dad's told me, and I think Pudge was the kindest name the kids threw at him. It stuck, even when he got to be a teenager and turned into a beanpole. He hasn't been able to shake the name. You know how it is with nicknames, how they stick?"

She cocked her head to one side as she watched him, one eyebrow arched in his direction. "You had one?"

"Yeah, I had one."

"What was it?"

"Oh, no," he said, shaking his head.

"Oh, another Pudge?"

"Not even close."

She studied him. "Stretch?" He shook his head. "Buddy?" He shook his head again. "Bubba?"

"No, not Bubba," he said on a chuckle. "How about you? Did you have a nickname?"

Her cheeks took on a blush of color at the question. "For a while."

"What was it?"

"If you won't tell, I won't tell," she said, the smile back and making his nerves tingle. "Tell me yours and I'll tell you mine?"

He shook his head. "No deal." He knew it was time to leave. This was feeling far too good and easy for him. "Now, I have to get going."

She frowned up at him. "For how long?"

"Until they need me to fill in."

"Okay," she breathed.

Why did he feel like some sort of ogre instead of a man doing his job, and not doing it very well? "Just let the officer on duty know what you need."

"Daddy! Daddy!"

He turned to see J.J. rushing into the lockdown area. He thought she'd left with Gen, but she was running right for his knees. He braced for impact, but she didn't make contact. Instead she neatly ducked around him and headed for Riley. She stopped and held up the sheet of paper he'd given her to scribble on. Even from the door, he could see the bright colors of a drawing.

He saw Riley's eyes widen as she looked at whatever was on the paper, then glance at him, high color in her cheeks. That's when he went into the cell. He crouched by J.J., and although what she'd drawn on the paper was only partially visible to him, he totally regretted her above-average artistic talents at that moment.

Even though the child had drawn a stick figure in her picture, there was no mistaking the figure was a woman, with huge blue eyes, red lips and bare feet, even if one foot looked as if it had six toes. The bars were unmistakable, too. Riley in her cell. Riley sitting in the corner with a bunch of blankets around her. Riley behind bars.

"Let me guess?" Riley said in a low voice. "That's me, isn't it?"

J.J. nodded vigorously. "Huh!"

"Well," she said, her eyes never leaving the drawing. "You've really captured the moment."

He didn't know who he was more worried for, the child who would be crushed if Riley didn't like her drawing, or the woman who'd lost all of her smiles at the sight of the crayon rendering.

"J.J.," he said, "you have to go home with Mamaw." He would have picked her up and taken her out, but right then Riley reached for the paper. He watched J.J. give the paper up willingly.

Riley held it as if it could burn her fingers. She stared at it for a long, awkward moment, then she looked at J.J. with eyes that were overly bright. He could handle pretty much anything except tears. Thankfully, there were no tears, just a weak smile and soft voice saying, "Thank you, it's really nice."

J.J. pointed to Riley with a grin. "Real pretty, huh?"

"Well, you made me look better than I really look," she said. "That means you're a great artist and I have a really nice gift."

J.J. suddenly moved, spinning around and running out of the cell, yelling for her mamaw.

Riley stared at the picture in her hand and had apparently almost forgotten that Joshua was still there until he spoke. "She's got this thing about drawing," he said.

She stared at the stick figure and said, "She's good." Too good. The picture made Riley feel more isolated than she had in a long time—and more discouraged about her situation. She didn't know why tears were so close to the surface at that moment, because she wasn't a weepy person usually, but when Joshua spoke to her, tears burned horribly behind her eyes.

"Are you okay?"

"Sure," she lied. "I'm not going to faint or throw up." She made herself look at Joshua who was still crouched by the cot and at her eye level. "Just—"

"Joshua!" someone called from the other room. "Detective Gagne from Chicago is on the line."

He looked at Riley, then stood and headed out of the cell. He didn't close the door, so she dropped the picture on her tray and went after him with her hopes starting to lift a bit. This could be the good news she needed so desperately. She hurried across the squad room, into his office, and stood right behind him when he reached for his telephone. "Pierce, here." He listened, then said, "Okay, I'll be here." And he hung up.

"What?" she asked. She knew she startled him by the way he turned quickly, hitting her in the arm with his elbow. She moved back, rubbing at the stinging in her upper arm, but not looking away from Joshua. "What did he say?" she asked.

"You're supposed to be in your cell," he said.

"You left the door open," she said with what she thought was real control at that moment. "Just tell me what he said."

He leaned back to half sit on the edge of the desk,

crossing his arms on his chest in the process. "They can't contact the owner, but he told a friend of his that it was stolen from his house."

Slowly she sank into a nearby straight-backed chair and stared at the floor. "Oh, shoot," she breathed, and hugged her arms around herself and tried to think, to figure out something, anything. "That's all the detective told you?"

"Everything."

Joshua was doing things most cops wouldn't do under any circumstances. But nothing he was doing made any difference. She bit her lip hard. "If...if I was set up," she said, still staring at the floor. "If they did this on purpose to get a stolen car to the West Coast..." She shivered and stopped her own words, then made herself look up at Joshua who hadn't moved from where he stood by the desk. "How can I prove it?"

His eyes met hers and she could see the answer in that gaze. He didn't have to say, "I don't know," for her to feel her stomach plunge and to realize that she was as close as she'd ever been to giving up. She couldn't prove anything. She'd been in the stolen car. She'd been the one driving. And she was the one about to be arrested.

She exhaled and made herself sit straighter, letting go of her grip on her middle. She closed her eyes for a moment, then looked up at Joshua. "I don't, either," she said flatly, and stood.

He studied her intently. "You really don't have anyone?"

"I told you. I don't have any family. I don't have a Gen or a J.J., or any people I know, not even a Pudge."

That sounded so self-pitying that it almost made her choke. "But, I am innocent," she said, exhaling again to try to clear her emotions and her thoughts. "And I will just have to figure it out."

He was there in front of her, close enough for her to see the pulse that beat at the base of his throat where the collar of his shirt parted, exposing a hint of dark chest hair. She looked up and she saw fine lines at the corners of his eyes, and it was then she realized he looked tired. Even though she'd seen the overall image at first, the freshly showered man, now he looked as if he hadn't slept at all last night.

"For what it's worth, I'll keep checking," he murmured.

"For what it's worth, thank you," she said, and moved around him, out of the office and back to the cell area. She was in the cell before she heard footsteps behind her. She turned, expecting to see Joshua, but found a lady dressed in a uniform-type skirt and shirt with a name badge that read, "Stella Myers." She slid the cell door shut and motioned to Riley's small table. "Breakfast's there. It just came in."

"Thanks." Then she saw the drawing beside the carry-out box of food.

"Call if you need anything else," Stella said, and left.

Riley sank onto the cot, leaned against the wall and pulled her legs up beneath her. She stared at the drawing without touching it. She heard footsteps again and looked up. This time she was surprised to see Gen standing there. She thought she'd left with J.J. "I'll be back tomorrow. Do you need me to bring you anything?"

"No, thanks," she said.

Gen came closer to the bars. "Riley, I'm good at reading people, and the one thing I know is, you don't belong here. If there's anything you can do to clear this up, you should, no matter who it affects."

Riley almost smiled. She'd do anything, but there wasn't anything. "If I knew a thing that would help, I'd do it. But I don't and I can't."

Gen shook her head. "I'm sorry." She glanced at the picture J.J. had drawn. "She's like her mommy, a real artist."

Riley found herself wondering what Joshua's wife had been like, a woman who had obviously been loved and had a family and friends and a place to be in the world. "She was talented?"

"Sarah? Very. I'm not sure J.J. even remembers her, but Sarah was terrific. She was kind and giving and—" She shrugged. "She was a very good woman."

A good woman. A fortunate woman. A talented woman. Obviously a much-loved woman. For a moment Riley was jealous of a dead woman, then it passed and she just felt empty inside.

Riley looked at the picture again. "Do you have some tape so I can hang this up on the wall?"

"Sure, I'll be right back," Gen said, and left.

Riley stared at the picture of her behind bars and she had to rub at her eyes. Life wasn't fair.

Gen returned and Riley hung up the picture on the wall above her cot. "Makes it downright homey," she murmured as she handed the tape back to Gen.

"Well, I wouldn't call it homey, but it does add a certain flair. Sarah once said she'd like to paint the walls yellow and put in window shades." She laughed again. "Now that would have been something."

"I don't know about yellow," Riley said, sitting on the cot. "There's not a jail cell in this country that yellow paint could improve."

"You've known a few cells?" Gen asked.

Riley frowned. "A couple."

"You know, Sarah was arrested once," she said in a hushed voice as if she'd dared to say the sun set in the east. "She was in a march in Washington, D.C. I remember Joshua calling and saying he was heading up to bail her out, and actually laughing about it. There he was, a cop bailing his wife out of jail, and he thought she was terrific for doing it."

She'd heard enough about Sarah. She didn't know why, but it thoroughly depressed her. She didn't want to ask the next question, but it came out anyway. "How did she die? Sickness or…?"

"Sarah wasn't sick a day in her life," Gen said, the smile gone now. "She was going to meet Joshua for dinner in the city, and J.J. was at home with Sarah's mother. Sarah never made it. Her car went off an overpass. Joshua sat at the restaurant for an hour before they contacted him." She shook her head. "It was horrible. Lots of press, of course, since Sarah was the only daughter of Sherman and Lorraine Ballew." She must have looked confused, because Gen said, "Very prominent people in Atlanta, both in finance and in society."

She'd never heard the names, but that didn't mean a thing.

She pressed her hands flat to the cot by her sides and pushed, letting her head fall back to look at the stark ceiling. She didn't want to talk about any of this, not Sarah or her lineage, and she closed her eyes tightly for a moment. "Life just does what life wants to do and we go along for the ride," she whispered.

"Are you quoting someone else or did you make that up?"

She was startled by Joshua's voice and she turned to see him watching her. "It's all mine," she muttered.

Gen looked from Joshua to Riley, then said, "I'm going." She touched Joshua on the shoulder. "See you soon?"

He nodded, but didn't look away from Riley. Gen left and Joshua stayed.

"No more news?" she asked, pressing her hands to her thighs.

He shook his head. "Nothing."

She exhaled. "So, where are you off to?"

"Home."

"Hey, Joshua?" It was Stella. "Call from the inn."

"What's up?"

"The big man says he needs you to swing past today around five to talk about the matter he spoke to you about yesterday."

"Tell him I'll be there," he said.

"'The big man'?" Riley asked.

"Jack Prescott. The guy I told you about who owns the inn."

"What's he like?" she asked, really wondering about this rich old friend of Joshua's.

"Jack's Jack. He's hard to explain if you haven't met him."

"The chance of me meeting your rich friend isn't

very good," she said, then she smiled slightly. "Un-less…?"

"Unless what?" he asked.

She scrambled off the cot and crossed to the secured cell door. "Could you take me with you when you go to see him?"

He looked as if she'd asked him to help her make a break for it. "What?"

"Take me with you." She knew her request was ridiculous and didn't stand a chance of being agreed on, but she didn't back down. "Just take me along, and let me meet your dear friend Jack, the rich man who owns most of this town." She held out her hands through the bars, almost touching him. "Handcuff me and let's go."

He stared at her, then quirked an eyebrow. "You're serious?"

"Absolutely," she said. "I'll never get another chance to meet someone like that, or to see this inn. I'll either be in San Diego or back in Chicago. This is my only chance."

He shook his head. "No, I'm going home for now, then I'll head out there later. I'll check on Chicago from home."

She knew what she'd asked was crazy, but the disappointment almost choked her. "Thanks," she muttered, and went back to the cot. She settled on the mussed blankets and heard Joshua leaving. It had been worth a try, and she'd never thought he'd agree to it, but she'd wanted to go, to get out of here again. She bit her lip. She wouldn't admit that she would have liked to have spent more time with Joshua.

She reached for the food container and settled in to spend the day waiting again. Lunch came and went, and the afternoon dragged by. Every noise from the outer room caught her attention, but Joshua never came back. He hadn't said he would, but she'd hoped he might.

She paced around the cell, then as the light from the single window began to fade, she went to the closed cell door and called, "Hello, out there!"

She expected Wes or Officer Todd to come in, or even sober-faced Stella, but it was Joshua who strode through the door. He was in the same casual clothes, but his jaw was vaguely shadowed with the beginnings of a new beard and his hair was mussed, as if he'd been raking his fingers through it. She hadn't heard him come in at all.

"You came back," was all she said.

"There was a problem," he said.

"Not something about me, was it?" she asked apprehensively.

"No, nothing to do with you. Not directly."

"What does that mean?"

"Do you still want to go with me to meet Jack?"

She knew her mouth probably fell in shock. She'd all but forgotten about her ridiculous request. She surely thought he had. "Are you kidding?" she asked.

"It's no joke," he said, and turned to the control board. She heard the click and reached for the barred door, then tugged it open.

When Joshua came back to her, she held out her hands to him. "Handcuffs?"

He exhaled as he shook his head. "No handcuffs."

She was surprised but didn't argue. "Okay."

His eyes flicked to her bare feet. "But you need boots."

"Yes, sir," she said, and turned, hurrying over to get her boots and push her feet into them. "So what is this place, like a fat farm or a place they hide out after plastic surgery or some kind of unofficial place where the rich and famous go to recover?" She went back to where he stood. "Or is it some sort of secret club?"

"It's a ski resort, and probably a rehab for a few."

"So just what does Rich Jack need from you?" she asked.

"I'll find out when I get there."

She didn't bother mentioning the fact that when he'd been told about the summons by Rich Jack, the wording had been, "that matter you'd discussed" or something along that line. But she wasn't about to question anything about this offer.

Chapter Ten

Riley wasn't taking any chances at all, and she hurried out of the lockdown, past Joshua and out into the squad room. When she entered, all three people in the space turned to look at her. Wes, Todd and Stella. None of them smiled. None of them said anything to her. They simply stared, then quickly went back to their conversation.

She had the most unsettling feeling that something was wrong. When she looked back at Joshua, she knew he was in on it. He didn't even look at the others who were making a show out of fixing some paper stacks on the desk they were standing beside.

She wanted out of here, no matter where she went, but she couldn't let it go. "What's wrong?" she asked.

"Nothing for you to worry about," was all he said before he went around her and crossed to a side desk. When he came back he had something faded and blue in his hand. Her jacket. "I got this out of the BMW for you." He held it out to her, but when she didn't move to take it, he moved closer. "Here. Put it on."

"Not until you tell me what's wrong," she said in a

low voice. The others were still making a show out of being busy, but she could feel them straining to hear what was being said.

What had existed between them earlier was gone, as was any connection she'd felt on their midnight walk. Now Joshua seemed tense and impatient. Her imagination was running wild and it was making her stomach hurt. Had they really heard from Chicago and he was taking her to the airport for extradition? Maybe he thought she'd freak out. Maybe he thought she'd faint again or throw up if she knew the truth. Whatever it was, she was the only one in the room who didn't know the truth.

"You know, I really want to meet Rich Jack and see this inn," she said, leaning closer and lowering her voice a bit. "But why are you so nervous?"

He exhaled roughly. "Just put on the jacket and we'll talk in the car."

His eyes held hers and she finally just gave in. She grabbed her jacket and put it on, then turned in a circle with her arms out. "Presentable?" she asked Joshua, but her voice was loud enough for all of them to hear.

"It's fine," he said, and took her by the arm to lead the way to the side exit. He pushed back the door and together they went out into the frigid late-afternoon air. They made their way to his car. But when she reached for the back door on the driver's side, Joshua stopped her.

"We're taking that," he said, motioning to a red SUV.

She skirted the back of the squad car and went

around to the passenger side of the SUV. It was customized, with chrome rims on huge wheels that gave a lot of road clearance to the chassis. The windows were tinted so dark that she couldn't see inside.

She opened the door and had to grab a chrome side rail to pull herself up onto the seat. As she settled on cold, gray-leather seats, Joshua went around and got behind the wheel, then turned on the engine. He let the big car idle while he flipped on the heater and put on his seat belt. Then he backed out and headed for the exit.

He pulled onto the main street, heading north, and obviously didn't intend to tell her anything, so she said, "Tell me what's going on."

Joshua had given up trying to understand the twists and turns his life seemed to take at the oddest moments. He just went with them and tried to cope as best he could. But he wasn't sure how much to tell Riley about why she was with him, so he stuck to the bare bones of the story. "They're bringing in some of the troublemakers at the public lifts. They're drunk and causing trouble. The staff tried to get them to back off, but they won't, so they're being brought in. They'll be held to sober them up, then given an escort out of town."

"What does that have to do with me?" she asked.

"We don't have private cells—you know that—and it was out of the question to have you in there with those animals."

"Why didn't you just handcuff me to a desk or lock me in your office?"

That's exactly what Charlie had said to do, and exactly what he hadn't wanted to happen. Their fight hadn't been explosive or even long. Charlie had accused him of being too close to the problem with Riley, and he'd accused Charlie of being too aggressive because of the upcoming election. Charlie's accusation about him had probably been right. His accusation about Charlie hadn't been. He owed the man an apology, but he'd do it later.

"There's no lock on the office, and I'm sure that handcuffing you to a desk for three or four hours would be a violation of something or other. Cruel and unusual."

"Why were the people in the squad room looking at us as if I had two heads?"

He didn't dare look at her, so he concentrated on the town as he passed the hotel, then headed for the public lifts. "They're stuck there, and you're going to meet Jack."

"Sure," she muttered. "And they're jealous?"

"Stranger things have happened," he murmured.

"You aren't going to tell me, are you?"

He felt her staring at him now. "I told you that—"

"Stop or I might have to make a citizen's arrest for felony lying."

He shook his head. "Okay, okay, I plead the Fifth. Let's change the subject."

"Okay, why don't you tell me what you're going to tell the people at this posh resort that Rich Jack owns about coming there with a prisoner?"

"I don't have to tell them anything," he said truthfully as they passed the crowds at the public ski lifts.

"What about Rich Jack? Does he know anything

about me?" She stopped him before he could answer. "Never mind. I know that he's probably sidled up to the pickle barrel at Ye Old General Store in town or gone to the barbershop and heard the gossip."

He could laugh at that, and he did. "I don't think I've ever seen a pickle barrel around here."

"Okay, maybe my arrest is the main topic around the hot tub at Rich Jack's fancy place? Conversation over cognac?"

Thankfully he spotted the rock fence that showed the beginnings of the property to the inn and slowed as he neared the main entrance. "First of all, Jack doesn't gossip, and second, let's stop calling him Rich Jack."

"Well, he's rich, isn't he?"

"He's just Jack," he murmured.

"And just rich?"

He glanced at her, his eyes narrowed so the impact of the smile on her face didn't hit him too hard. Damn it, she was beautiful when she smiled. Hell, she was beautiful anytime. Charlie had said he was too involved with her case, but if the truth were told, it wasn't her case that kept her in his thoughts. He slowed and turned to enter the massive wooden gates that guarded the privacy of everything and everyone at the inn.

"'The Inn at Silver Creek,'" Riley read from the intricate brass sign set in the stone pillars as the guard came out of the guardhouse.

He came toward the car, bundled in a dark jacket with fur trim and a snug fur hat to fight against the cold. Joshua rolled down his window just enough to speak to him. "Hey, Ryce."

"He's expecting you," the middle-aged man said before he turned and went back to the guardhouse. A moment after he stepped inside, the massive gates slowly opened and Joshua drove on through toward the sprawling, multifloored main lodge. The stone-and-wood structure went out of sight in either direction, and huge pines framed the front valet area. A huge portico shot out from a snow-heavy roof that was at least two stories high, protecting the arriving guests who approached the sweep of stone stairs at the main entry.

"So Rich Jack is expecting you, is he?"

"Jack. Just Jack," he muttered as he slowed. "This is a small town, or at least it was a small town, and there was one school, and Jack and I hung out together. He's just Jack."

"The rich kid and the sheriff's kid?"

"And the kid from the orphanage, Cain Stone. Even Doc—Gordie—was part of my childhood." He stopped the SUV by a private entrance almost hidden behind a partial stone wall on the side of the main level. He pulled into an unmarked spot beside Jack's Porsche.

He got out, but heard her say just before he closed the door, "The Cain Stone who owns the Dream Catcher Hotel and Casino?"

He went around to her side and met her by the front of the SUV as she hunched into the wind. "Yes, that Cain Stone. And, yes, he's rich, too. And he's a friend."

"Sure," she said, then looked away from him. "Where to now?"

"Inside, out of this cold," he said, and walked toward the partial stone wall with her following him.

He reached into his pocket and used his security card to enter the building. She went inside with him, but he stopped her before they went any farther into the back hallway.

"Just remember, his name's Jack. Okay?"

She stopped and turned to him, smiling, an expression that always took him by surprise and made it exceptionally hard to breathe. "Sticks and stone will—"

"Forget it," he said, and turned away to head down the hall.

The sound of his boots on the worn stone floors echoed off the wood-paneled walls where old lanterns wired for electricity cast a soft glow over everything. Christmas music, mixed with distant laughter, drifted on the warm air, and he realized how luxurious this must all seem to Riley. He was used to it. He had been here when this had all been new. He stopped by the private elevator, pushed his access card into the security slot and the single door opened immediately.

They both stepped inside the mirrored car and a silence hung between them. Then he turned, hit the button and, as the door slid silently shut, faced Riley's reflection. Those eyes were holding his in the mirror, and she finally spoke. "No floor numbers?"

"It only goes to one floor," he murmured.

"A private elevator for…Jack."

Riley glanced away from Joshua's reflection and looked at her own. From the faded jeans to the jacket with the cuffs starting to show wear, she didn't fit at this luxurious place. But oddly, Joshua seemed to, despite his casual clothes. She chanced a quick look back at him and met his narrowed eyes, intense in their scrutiny of her.

She found herself saying, "I promise, I'll behave," and making an exaggerated cross-my-heart motion with her hand on her chest.

She thought he was going to laugh at that, and she wished he would. But it never happened because the elevator stopped right then and the door slid open.

Riley had expected luxury, but she truly hadn't had a clue what form that luxury would take. Now she faced it and could barely take it in. They'd stepped into a grand room, done in rich, deep leathers, lush fabrics framing a wall of windows to her left, a massive stone fireplace to the right, and heavy gold chandeliers hanging from rugged beams overhead. In another incarnation, it would have been the entrance to an office. In this incarnation, it was a plush sitting room, complete with a wall of books bound in leather, a rosewood desk to the left holding a sleek computer along with crystal balls in a glass basket and a telephone with so many buttons it could have controlled a jet plane. The room was empty.

"Jack?" Joshua called.

There was a thump, then a door she hadn't seen opened. A man came out and she didn't have to ask anyone to know he was Rich Jack. He was an angular man with almost shoulder-length dark hair peppered with gray, dressed in well-worn jeans, an open-necked chambray shirt and what looked like scuffed leather boots. He was rich enough to dress down and still look impressive.

He spotted Joshua and the two men stepped toward each other, hands held out, the handshake firm as they met, the other hands clapping the other's shoulder.

"Good to see you," Jack said, then glanced past Joshua at Riley. "And you're not alone."

Riley braced herself and went closer to the two men. "I'm Riley Shaw." The smile faltered just a bit and she knew that he recognized the name. Whether it was around a pickle barrel or a hot tub, he knew who she was and had been told what she'd done.

"I'm Jack Prescott."

She shrugged. "And you own this whole place and most of the town, the pickle barrels and the hot tubs?"

He frowned at her. "What?"

"Nothing," Joshua said. "Did you get some news?"

He glanced at Riley, then back to Joshua. "We need to talk." He motioned to Riley. "Do you want her out here or inside?"

Riley felt her skin burn. "Let's make this simple and he can chain me to the fireplace." She didn't care when she heard Joshua exhale with obvious exasperation, even though Jack laughed as if she'd made a joke. She didn't feel funny right then.

"Whatever works," he said, then turned to head back to the door. "I'll be inside waiting."

She'd been stupid enough to think that even if he knew who she was, he'd act civilly toward her. Stupid, she thought. "He thought I was kidding," she said in a hissing whisper to Joshua. "Get out your handcuffs and go ahead and chain me to something that I can't steal." She held out her right hand, wrist up to Joshua. "Damn, I never should have come. I would have had a better time with drunk skiers than this."

Joshua moved closer, and she pressed her hand to his chest. But he didn't look down at it. He never looked away from her face. When he spoke, he was so close that the heat of his breath brushed her face. "It's my fault. They told me not to bring you," he said in a low voice.

She didn't understand. "What?"

"All of them—Charlie, the others—they told me not to bring you with me, that I was getting too involved in…everything."

She felt her face flame. That's why they'd stared at her like that. They thought the poor widower was being taken in by a car thief. More gossip for them to share. She couldn't even begin to think what they were saying right now. "They went off together, you know." Or "She was wearing his jacket the other night, out on the streets at midnight." She had to swallow hard to speak. "You should have listened to them and left me chained to a desk, then you could have visited Rich Jack on your own."

He came even closer and her hand was caught between the two of them, his heart beating rapidly against her palm. "No, I shouldn't have," he murmured, and caught her chin with his hand, making her look right at him. "I wanted you to come with me."

She could feel her eyes burning. "Why?"

He started to say something, then stopped, and she felt an unsteadiness in his touch when his lips found hers. At first she couldn't move. She couldn't even think. The world was at a standstill. She felt his heart hammering against her hand and his breath invading her, his other hand on her back, pulling her against him. She knew that she'd wanted to hug him before when he'd talked Charlie into giving her a break. Now she just wanted him. She wanted his touch. She wanted his taste. She wanted to let time stop, to push away reason and to just exist in the moment. His heat was everywhere and she felt as if his essence was filtering into her world, into her soul. It was remarkable and unlike anything she'd ever felt before.

HE'D WANTED HER to come with him. A stark truth. And Joshua knew the truth in it when he touched Riley, then tasted her. It was insanity. Definitely. And probably a huge dose of being alone for far too long. A rebound kind of thing, Stella had said. But he didn't know. All he knew was he tasted her and felt her body mold to his. He felt as if an ache he'd thought was permanently burned into his soul was beginning to heal. Bit by bit. With each breath of hers he inhaled. With the way her arms lifted and circled his neck. With the feeling of her breasts against his chest.

"Joshua!" He was startled by Jack calling out to him from the other room and the way everything shattered at the sound. "Lock her up or bring her in here, but let's get this show on the road."

Reluctantly he pulled back, lifting his hands to frame her face and to keep that connection a moment longer. He looked down into her flushed face and trembled when her tongue touched her lips. He could taste her in his mouth and he didn't want to lose that, any more than he wanted to lose what was happening between them.

"What—" she whispered.

"Shh," he breathed, moving to touch her lips with his forefinger. "Later. We'll talk," he said.

Thankfully she didn't demand answers there and then, because he knew that any explanation he could give her would only be more confusing. Instead she simply nodded, then turned and headed for the inner door. She went inside and he heard her say, "So, this is your home?"

He exhaled, shaking off the images and sensations that bombarded him. He went after her, half expecting her to be toe-to-toe with Jack. But she was just inside the door, quite deliberately looking around the space that looked like a very expensive hotel suite. It was cut into multilevels, partly used for sitting, partly for enjoying the view from a series of French doors that opened onto a private balcony, and partly for sitting in front of a fireplace that duplicated the one in the entry area.

He watched her look off to the left, through double doors and up a level, where there was the bedroom suite, boasting, Joshua knew, a sunken tub that sat in marble in front of windows that had an unobstructed view of the best ski run at the inn. There was also a shower that was wall-less, with a water supply that looked like a waterfall set in stone. If she saw that, she'd really say something. As it was, he could almost hear her thinking, *Rich Jack. Very Rich Jack.* And he waited for her to say that very thing. But she didn't.

Jack said, "Sit down and take off your jackets," and motioned them to the two ox-blood leather sofas that faced each other in front of the raised stone hearth of the fireplace. She headed for the nearest couch, slipped off her jacket and dropped it on the couch arm before she sat on the plush leather.

Joshua followed suit, laying his jacket over hers, but he couldn't sit close to her right then. So he went past her and sat on the raised hearth with the last remnants of a fire at his back. Jack sat opposite Riley, leaned forward and clasped his hands loosely together as he looked at Joshua.

"Cain still hasn't shown up," Jack said to Joshua.

Cain had been expected at the inn two days ago, but when he hadn't made it, Joshua hadn't been too concerned. Cain had always marched to his own drummer. "And that's a problem because…?" he asked, aware of Riley sitting quietly, her hands clasped in her lap.

"He's not at the Dream Catcher, and everyone there thinks he's here. His cell goes right to voice mail and he hasn't called in to anyone, including me."

Cain hadn't wanted to come to the inn in the first place, Joshua knew, and it wasn't unusual for him to go missing. "Did you check with that Ashley?"

"They're over and done. According to her, they haven't been together for a couple of months."

"I didn't know," Joshua admitted, but he wasn't surprised that the current lady in Cain's life was no longer current. "Was he flying in or driving?"

"Driving."

"People can fly here?" Riley asked, catching both men's attention.

Joshua saw her lean forward with curiosity. "The inn has a helicopter pad that some guests use in the nicer weather."

"Oh, sure, yeah," she said, giving him a look before she sat back. "Of course."

Jack seemed oblivious to the tinge of sarcasm in her

tone, but it didn't escape Joshua. "What was he driving?" he asked, focusing on Jack again.

"A new car, an SUV of some sort. He took off late in the afternoon two days ago."

"What do you want me to do?"

He glanced at Riley, then at Joshua. "If you can find the time, maybe you can make a few calls. Check with your connections."

The remark was pointed about his time and he just hoped Riley hadn't caught it. "I can ask around."

Jack took a slip of paper out of his shirt pocket and tossed it across to Joshua, letting it land on a huge leather ottoman that stood between the two couches. "No license plates, but it has dealer's paper plates from Vegas. That's the year, model, make and dealer information."

Joshua grabbed the paper, glanced at it and stuffed it into his shirt pocket. "So your friend just disappeared?" Riley asked. Jack looked at her with a degree of impatience, but she obviously noticed it. "He just walked out of the casino and no one's seen him since?"

"Looks that way," Jack said tightly.

She kept going. "Why would he do that?"

"I don't know," Jack said.

"Did he have problems?" she asked.

"I don't know that, either," Jack said curtly, and turned toward Joshua, cutting Riley off. "Are you going to look for him?" he asked.

"Sure, I'll look for him, but my gut reaction is, he's just being Cain and doing his own thing. You'll probably find him with some showgirl from the revue at the casino, and he won't thank us one bit, but I'll do it."

"Excuse me?" Riley said.

Jack turned to her. "What now?"

Jack had always been blunt. He didn't play the games most men in his position did. But at that moment, Joshua wished he'd lighten up a bit. He didn't miss the way color stained Riley's cheeks. "I just wondered where your bathroom is?"

"Right through there." Jack motioned to the bedroom suite. "Go through the doors, to the right, up a step and through the arch."

"Thanks," she said, and glanced at Joshua before she hurried toward the doors.

Jack didn't say a thing for a long moment after Riley left, but Joshua did. "You don't have to treat her like some sort of plague," he said.

Jack lifted one eyebrow at him. "What?"

"Cutting her off, acting as if she's being a pest when she's just asking smart questions."

Jack sat back, clasped his hands behind his head and let out a puff of air. "I'm not the one who should be on the spot for the way I'm treating her."

"What does that mean?"

"I went out to get you, to talk about the skiers making trouble, and you were all over her."

Joshua stood, but Jack stayed on the couch, looking up at him. "Who in the hell do you think you are?"

He sat forward, his eyes holding Joshua's. "I'm your friend. I want you to have a life, to get on with things, but not this way. And not with this woman."

Chapter Eleven

Riley heard the voices when she got back to the door that led to Jack's living area. She'd almost gotten lost in the gigantic bathroom, but Joshua's voice caught her attention as she reached to pull the door open and stopped it at an inch or so.

He was angry. "What are you talking about?"

"I'm not against you finding someone. God knows, you need to start your life again, but they said you arrested her in a hundred-and-thirty-thousand-dollar car that was stolen from some guy in Chicago. She's rootless, and you don't know a damn thing about her. What are you thinking?" She heard a jarring chuckle. "Never mind. I know what you're thinking about, and that's okay. A little fun. A little relaxation. As long as that's all there is to it and Charlie or your dad don't find out."

Riley closed her eyes so tightly colors exploded behind them. To have this man who had treated her like some common criminal lay it out like that made her physically sick. "You always cut to the lowest possible denominator, don't you, Jack?"

"You aren't saying you think you love her, are you?"

"Love? We aren't talking about love."

"Whew, thank God for lust. Pure and simple lust."

"You should know," Joshua said with a touch of humor in his voice.

Riley felt light-headed, as if the world was receding and she had a panicked moment when she thought she might faint again. She'd never fainted and here she was, going two for two with Joshua. But it didn't happen. Love. She sucked in a deep breath. No, that wasn't what this was about. But it wasn't pure and simple, either. Not for her. Not when the man could rock her world with his touch.

She caught her breath, steadied herself and realized that she wanted to go back to jail. That had to be a first for her, wanting to go to jail. But she wanted out of here. The door moved without warning, swinging back toward her, striking her hand before it was open. Joshua stood in front of her. Lust. Yes, lust. That's what she felt for him when he'd kissed her. That had to be it. Love was out of the question. "Ready to leave?" Joshua asked.

"Yes," she said, and went past him, being careful not to make any contact. She crossed to the couch, picked up his jacket, then hers and turned to hold his out to him. He took it and turned to her, but before he could say anything else, a phone rang.

She glanced in the direction of the sound and saw Jack take a cell phone from his pocket and flip it open. He held up a hand to keep Joshua and her there while he answered it. "Yes?"

He listened, then said, "You could have called before this." He listened for a long moment before speaking again. "Sure, of course. When?" He nodded. "Good. Make sure you're here then. I'll have everything ready. Oh, are you coming by yourself?"

He nodded at what the person on the other end of the line said. "Smart man," he murmured, then, "Be here," and hung up.

"What's going on?" Joshua asked.

"That was Cain. He says he got sidetracked with a supplier." He shrugged. "He'll be here next week."

"Good," Joshua said, then looked at Riley. "Let's go."

Jack spoke up. "What about the skiers?"

He was speaking to Joshua. "Right." Then Joshua turned to her. "Can you wait outside for me?"

"You're telling me to wait outside by myself?"

He shrugged. "You don't have the card key for the elevator. You can't go anywhere."

She looked away from him to glance at Jack, and lied through her teeth. "Nice to meet you." She left the room and reached to pull the door shut behind her. It closed with a satisfying click and blocked out the two men behind her.

Riley paced nervously around the outer room, then finally stopped at the elevator. A key card? She looked around the door, but there was no slot for any card. She hit the call button. The door slid open and she glanced inside. No key card slot in there, either, just the single button to go down.

She moved back, let the door slide shut and shook her head. Did he think she was stupid? No, she was someone to lust after and a car thief who would take off at a moment's notice. That put it in perspective. She had an urge to get on the elevator and just go away. But she had nowhere to go.

She crossed to the windows and looked out at the world of the rich at the inn. The main cabins that were scattered around the grounds, the network of ski lifts that were moving even with no one on them. She noticed a handle on the nearest window in the right corner and touched it. It clicked and a section of windows structured like a French door opened and led out onto a small balcony suspended over the life below.

She glanced back at the closed door to Jack's suite, then stepped out into the biting cold of early evening. She couldn't run anywhere, but she could get outside. She closed the door behind her and crossed the six-foot expanse to a high wooden railing. The sun was just setting, falling behind the mountains to the west in a splash of vibrant colors that flowed over the snowy land. The air was bitterly cold, but it felt good to be outside. It helped clear her head. Then again, maybe that was happening because Joshua wasn't around.

She frowned, then touched her lips with the tips of her fingers, remembering the kiss, then Joshua saying, "We'll talk." She had a feeling she knew what that talk would be about, especially after his private conversation with Jack. Jack had cut to the chase, said things in a bleak, obvious way. A car thief. Lust. Just a little fun. But what he hadn't said, and what she'd heard loud and clear was, she wasn't Sarah. She wasn't even close. She was someone you had fun with, then left without looking back. Not someone who you stayed with and loved and…

Riley bit her lip, hard. Joshua was lonely, she knew that. He still grieved for his wife. What happened with them was something basic, an impulsive thing. God knew, she felt that basic response to him. Right or wrong. She'd never felt as drawn to a man as she was to Joshua. That made her shiver and it had nothing to do with the cold surrounding her. It was the cold in her soul. That emptiness that she'd always known was there, but was forgotten every time Joshua touched her.

If she could, if she was capable of being more than she was, she could love Joshua. That admission stunned her. Love? She didn't even know what that meant. She'd thought it was something others felt and something she'd never know. She never had. But now, she knew with a certainty that if life had dealt her a different hand, she might have found out what love was or could be.

She hugged herself more tightly and turned to go back inside, but stopped when she saw Joshua through the wavy glass, heading for the elevator. His image was distorted, but that didn't diminish the impact of what she'd been thinking. And it hurt her soul. He turned, saw her outside, then strode toward the door and jerked it open.

He didn't step outside, but remained standing in the doorway. "What are you doing?" he demanded abruptly.

He'd thought she'd run. He always thought she'd run. She knew it shouldn't sting, that it made perfect sense for him not to trust her, but it did sting. He'd even lied to her about some stupid key card. "Getting fresh air," she said in a voice that was edged with an anger she felt at herself. He didn't move, so she went toward him and was thankful when he stepped aside to let her back inside.

They made their way to the elevator and stepped inside before the door slid shut. The car started its descent and she caught his eye in the reflection off the door.

She averted her eyes, staring down at the floor, at her boots next to his. "Sorry about making you wait," he said.

She shrugged. "I've got nothing but time."

"Riley, listen. I need to explain something to you."

Oh, no, he didn't. She wasn't going to stand here and hear him go on about how mistakes are made, how fun is fun, lust is lust. She'd had enough of that for one day. "No, you don't," she said.

"I do."

She lifted her eyes to his reflected gaze. "No, you don't," she said. When he would have said something else, she said quickly, "There's nothing to talk about. Nothing, unless Rich Jack has another problem besides annoying skiers I should know about?"

His eyes narrowed and she could almost see him wondering what she knew, what she'd heard. But she wasn't going to tell him. "You heard. Cain's coming in a few days."

"Yeah, I heard," she said, and looked away to stare at the mirrored surface of the elevator door. She felt the car stop, but when the door should have opened, they didn't. Jack had his thumb pressed against the "door closed" button.

"Do you have a problem?" he asked, and she thought that was the most ludicrous question she'd ever heard.

A problem? Everything about him was a problem for her. From the way just seeing him made her heart race, to the way he had of making her breath catch just by looking at her. "Just going back to jail," she said.

He stared at her, as if trying to make up his mind about something, then he let go of the button and the door slid silently open.

She stepped out and quickly headed for the door where they'd come in. Then Joshua was there, reaching around her to push the door open and she felt his body against hers for a fleeting moment. She quickly stepped into the frigid air.

Night had fallen quickly and the sky was black, showing no stars. She heard someone laughing in the distance, the opening and closing of car doors, Christmas music and the ever-present scent of smoke in the air. She hurried down the steps, over to the red SUV and went around to get inside. She settled on the cold leather, put on her seat belt, then pushed herself into the corner, as far from Joshua as she could get at that moment.

Moments later they were approaching the gates. They swung back slowly as the SUV exited. As Joshua stopped at the highway to turn right, a phone rang. He pulled aside and answered it.

"Yes?" He didn't say anything else as he listened, but Riley didn't miss a growing tightness in his expression. Finally he said, "I'm on my way," and flipped the phone

shut. He dropped it on the console between them, then
swung north, away from town. "That was Gen."

For some reason, she felt her stomach tighten. "Is
it something with J.J.?"

He shook his head. "No, it's Dad."

Even though she hadn't met his father, her stomach tightened even more. "His heart?"

"No, his stubbornness. He's insisting on clearing
snow by the barn, and he can't use the blower there. It's
too rocky. Gen's worried about him going out and doing
it."

"I've heard that heart patients shouldn't shovel
snow at all. Something about the cold and the exer-
tion."

"You know it, and I know it, and Gen knows it, but
Dad's insisting." He drove farther north, away from
Silver Creek and the skiing crowds.

"Where is this ranch?" she asked, looking around
at the snowy night.

"A half mile and we're there," he said.

The road had been cleared, but it was bumpy, and
she was glad when he slowed again at a rough stone
arch heavy with snow. She assumed there had to be a
gate in the arch, but it was open and out of sight. He
pulled through the entry where the path was snowy
and no drive clearly defined. But Joshua knew where
he was going and the SUV made it easily as they
climbed. They crested the hill and she was presented
with a night scene that looked like something right out
of a Christmas card.

An almost-full moon had risen and bathed the
scene in a cool light. She could see what had to be the

main structure, a sprawling two-story building that was totally outlined in multicolored Christmas lights; the peaks of the roof, the lines of two side wings and an entry where the lights had changed to blue. Off to the right in the distance, were two more buildings, smaller, but framed in lights, too.

Joshua slowed the car, then pulled in toward the house. The lights danced off the snow and the smoke from a central chimney rose into the night air. "We're here," he said, turning off the engine and reaching for his door. "You'd better come in."

She didn't hesitate. She was out by the time he came around to her door, and followed him to the blue glow of what she could see now was a full porch. He entered the house first, and she followed into warmth and brightness.

The house was laid out simply, with a huge room in the middle, centered around a brick fireplace that held a blazing fire. Comfortable, well-worn furniture filled the space, and a staircase led up to the next floor. To the left was a dining area and beyond that a kitchen. To the right, she could make out a library of sorts, a room filled from floor to ceiling with books. A huge Christmas tree stood against the back wall in front of a bank of windows.

Gen came down the stairs carrying J.J. The little girl squealed when she saw Joshua and by the time Gen was at the bottom of the stairs, Joshua was reaching for the diving J.J. The little girl hugged him fiercely, then glanced at Riley. She looked surprised for a moment, then she grinned.

"What a nice surprise," Gen said, catching Riley off guard when she reached out and gathered her in a tight hug. Then she stood back and glanced at Joshua. "You finally let the poor thing out."

"Just for a while," he said as J.J. twisted to get down.

He crouched to put her on the floor and she took off toward the kitchen. "Where is he?"

Gen exhaled and her smile started slipping. "He's throwing a fit in the study, and I think you're the only one who can talk sense to him." She was obviously exasperated as she motioned to the right wing.

Joshua glanced at Riley, then back to Gen. "Can you get Riley something to eat while I go and see him?"

Riley started to object, but Gen had her by her arm before she could say anything. "Of course. We've got plenty of food as long as you like spaghetti."

She nodded as Joshua headed off to see his dad. "Sure, that's fine. I practically live on pasta."

"Great, great," Gen said, and led her in the same direction J.J. had gone.

"Sit," Gen instructed when they reached the kitchen.

Riley did as she was told and then complimented Gen on the kitchen's decor.

"It was my only condition for marrying Joshua's father. A new kitchen." She was at the refrigerator and her voice was slightly muffled when she ducked behind the door to look inside. "I hated the old one. It was tiny, with no counter space and a stove barely big enough to boil water on." She stepped back and swung the door shut. "So I had it redone."

She brought out two covered dishes and crossed to the counter by the sinks. "It's huge," Riley said.

"That's the point. Really big. Lots of room. All the modern conveniences." She took a plate out of the upper cupboards, worked for a moment in silence, then turned and opened a microwave over the counter. She slipped the plate in, set the timer and started the microwave. She turned to Riley. "I love that. Heat things up in a minute or two, piping hot."

That was all Riley had used for years, an old microwave in her one-room apartment. "They're a modern miracle."

When the microwave beeped, Gen brought the food over to Riley. "How about some wine?"

Riley hesitated. "I'm not sure I should."

Gen shook her head. "Sweetie, you're in our home and you're our guest. Forget about the jail."

She wished she could. "Some wine sounds wonderful."

Gen went about getting wine out of a side cupboard, then poured a goblet for Riley and one for herself. She sat across the island from Riley and lifted her glass. "Merry Christmas, Riley Shaw."

She lifted her goblet. "Merry Christmas," she murmured, and took a sip of the smooth red wine.

Gen took a sip, then sighed. "It wasn't an easy thing to do, not when Joshua's mother, Mary, had worked in the old kitchen for years and I'm sure never complained a bit. She was great, from all I've heard. Giving, kind, loving." She smiled. "I thought it would be a hard act to follow, to be honest."

"Was it?" Riley asked, cradling her wine goblet.

"Yes and no. It took me a while to realize that I was Gen and she was Mary, and we both loved the same man at different times in life. Mary was perfect for her time with Noah, and I'm grateful for my life with Noah now." She drank more wine, then grinned. "So far, it's terrific, even if he's a stubborn old coot."

"Mamaw!"

J.J. burst into the kitchen on a dead run from a side room and headed for the island where the two women sat. But she didn't go to Gen. Instead she came around to Riley and held up a sheet of paper. "Here," she said, holding it for Riley to take.

"For me?"

"Huh!" she said with a vigorous shake of her head.

Riley took it, hesitating, then looked at it. But this time the drawing wasn't of a stick person behind bars. This time it was a stick figure in front of a huge Christmas tree with other stick figures. She didn't have to ask to know the one beside her was Joshua, taller and more solid-looking, and the two sitting on a rough couch had to be Gen and Noah. It looked like a family. She was in it, just on paper and in a small child's imagination, but for that moment, she was part of a real family.

JOSHUA STEPPED into the kitchen to find Gen and Riley at the island, and J.J. looking up at Riley who was holding a sheet of paper. Another drawing. He didn't want to deal with this now, not after his argument with his father. Then he realized that Riley was almost smiling this time. "Wow," she said softly, looking at the picture, then at J.J. "This is beautiful."

J.J. grinned, obviously pleased at Riley's reaction.

After the last drawing, he was anxious to see what J.J. had come up with this time. "Like it?" J.J. asked as he got closer.

"I—I love it."

J.J. clapped her hands together. "More pictures," she announced, and ran off to the playroom Gen had set up by the kitchen.

Joshua watched.

Riley put the paper on the island and reached for her glass of wine. Her hand wasn't very steady when she lifted the goblet and took a quick sip. He moved closer and looked down at the picture. All of them, including Riley. All of them, and no bars. He breathed a silent sigh of relief as he glanced at Riley who had turned to pick up her fork and poke at the steaming plate of spaghetti.

"Do you want some food?" Gen asked him.

He nodded. "Sure." He took the stool next to Riley and didn't miss the slight paleness in her cheeks.

"Are you okay?" he asked.

Her fork stilled as she cast him a sideways glance that was shadowed by her lowered lashes. "Fine," she whispered.

Gen put a plate in front of him, then laid out the silverware before heading to the cupboard and saying over her shoulder, "I'll get you some wine. You're not on duty."

He didn't respond to her, but kept looking at Riley. She was back to her food, finally spooling some noodles onto her fork. She ate a bit, but put the rest of it back on her plate. "You don't have to eat if you don't want to. Gen won't be offended."

"Good gracious, no, I won't be offended," Gen said as she put a plate of food in front of Joshua along with a glass of wine.

"Maybe we should be going back to the jail?" Riley suggested.

He checked his watch. "I think we need to give Todd another hour to clear the cells."

"Fine," she murmured, and turned, reached for her glass of wine and drank the last of it. Then she turned to her spaghetti and methodically began cutting it into small segments with the fork.

Gen sat opposite them, nursing her glass of wine. When she caught Joshua's eye, she nodded toward Riley and lifted an eyebrow in question. There was no way he could tell her what was going on, because he didn't understand it. The kiss had been mutual, and not broken by either one of them by choice. But right now, he felt closer to Riley than he ever had been to anyone in his life. That thought stopped him. She was in his life? He conceded that she was very much in his life. He just didn't know where things would lead.

"That's a great picture J.J. drew," he said to interrupt his thoughts.

Riley kept cutting the spaghetti. "She's a great artist."

"Sarah was a wonderful artist, too," Gen said. "She had a showing once in one of the best galleries in Atlanta. Just beautiful work."

Joshua saw the way Riley stopped cutting her food and started spearing the small pieces. "Sarah could do just about anything, couldn't she?" Riley asked, staring at the food on her fork.

"Well, yes, she was very…"

Joshua shot Gen a look that cut off her words. He didn't want to be talking about Sarah right now. "This is great spaghetti," he said, twirling his fork to catch the noodles. "Really good."

Riley ate a bit, but he could tell it was a token thing for her, and to be honest, he'd lost his appetite, too. When she pushed back her plate, he did the same thing. He took out his cell phone and called in to the station to find out how things were going. The good news was the troublemakers were leaving town, but the bad news was they had their stuff at the inn. They'd sent Wes to get their things, but it would be another hour before they were out of town and the jail was clear.

He hung up, then looked at Riley as Gen removed their plates.

Riley slipped off her stool and he did the same. "Why don't we sit in the living room for a bit before starting back?" He reached for her wineglass and for his. "I'll get some more wine and be right in."

She went around him and out of the kitchen. He looked at Gen who was turning to look at him. "That poor thing," Gen said. "I thought that picture from J.J. would cheer her up." She left the rinsed plates stacked on the counter and wiped her hands on a dish towel. "You know she doesn't belong in that jail. Stop being a lawman for a few minutes and look at her as a human being."

He almost laughed. That would be his downfall, when she went from being a suspect to being… He couldn't even find a word for what happened to him when he looked at Riley or when he touched her or kissed her. Jack had called it lust, but he'd known even then that it was more. He just didn't know what to call it.

Or maybe he didn't want to admit the truth—even to himself.

Chapter Twelve

By the time Joshua got into the living room, Riley was sitting facing his father on the sofas by the fireplace. They both glanced at him as he walked in and then went back to their conversation. Gen headed out to get J.J.

Joshua heard his father laughing when he crossed to sit on the same sofa as Riley. He placed both their wineglasses on the big coffee table in front of them. Noah Pierce looked remarkably healthy for having survived a heart attack just four months ago. His hair was salt and pepper, but thick, and his tanned skin didn't have that ashen look it had when Joshua had seen him in the hospital. His dad was his size, a bit heavier, but a man who had worked hard all his life, and when he'd had a heart attack, he'd felt betrayed by his body.

"So, Josh lit the fire in the wash bucket to warm up and before he knew it, the fire found the hay and…" His dad shrugged. "As they say, the rest was a raging bonfire."

"In my defense," Joshua said, sitting forward, "I

was only ten, and the consensus was it would warm up the stable."

Riley laughed at that. "The consensus?"

His dad cut in. "Jack, Cain and Gordie. You never knew what they'd get into when they were together."

"Well, we sure weren't trying to burn down the place."

"Heaven help us if you wanted to burn it down," his father said, barely suppressing a chuckle.

"But, we didn't."

"Absolutely," his dad said, and stood, stretching his arms over his head as Gen came in with J.J. in her arms. They were bundled up, ready to leave, and that was when Joshua remembered the pageant. The practice was tonight, the procession of the torches, and Charlie dressed as Santa would lead the way down the ski slope.

His dad looked at him. "Come on. We gotta get going."

"We're not going," he said quickly, ignoring Riley's inquisitive look.

"Okay," he said, then smiled at Riley. "Nice to meet you." He looked back at his son. "And you be sure that the snow gets cleared?"

"Absolutely, Dad. Tomorrow, first thing."

Gen was looking at the two of them while she tried to control a bouncing J.J. in her arms. "Are you sure you two can't come along?"

Joshua shook his head. "No, we can't."

"Come on, Gen, we need to get a move on," Noah said, and she smiled at the two of them. J.J. waved, and the three were gone. When the door closed, Joshua sank back on the couch and felt Riley's gaze on him.

"Where aren't we going?" she asked.

"To see the practice for the procession of torches. The Christmas pageant Charlie's in."

She stood abruptly. "Take me back to the station and just chain me up somewhere, then you can go with your family to the pageant rehearsal." She looked around, but never at him. "Where's the restroom?"

"There's one back off the kitchen, through the playroom and off the bedroom, but you don't have—"

He was speaking to her back as she disappeared. Joshua sat there for a long moment, heard a door close, then the rumble of running water through the pipes of the old house. He waited several minutes, then got up and headed back to find Riley, making his way to the back of the house and to his old bedroom.

Riley stood there, beside the old oak bureau that sat opposite the twin-size bed. She was holding a picture in her hands, staring at it. She turned toward him and held up the framed print. "The four of you?" she asked.

He crossed to her and looked down at the four boys in the picture, Cain, Jack, Gordie and himself in ski togs. All of them had changed so much in the twenty-five years since the picture was taken. "That's us."

"Before or after the arson incident?" she asked with the shadow of a smile that knotted tension in his neck.

He flexed his arms to try to ease it. "After. We're twelve or so in that shot. The barn fire was a few years earlier." He ran a hand around his neck, pressing at the tightness there. "And the barn didn't burn. It smoldered."

"Oh, great distinction," she said as she put the picture back on the bureau and turned to face the rest of the room. "This room looks as if it goes back at least twenty-five years, too."

"Thirty-seven years, as long as I've been around." He glanced at the plaid spread on the single bed and the trophies on the shelves along with dog-eared books and old board games. It seemed odd to have her in here, to see what he was so many years ago, but on the other hand, he didn't want to leave the room. He didn't want her to leave the room.

"Years and years and years?" she murmured.

"Okay, I'm old, but not that old." He flicked her chin with the tip of his fingers and the slight contact jolted through him. He stepped back and cupped the nape of his neck, pressing at the knotted muscles.

He must have grimaced, because she came closer and looked up at him. "Your neck?"

"It's tight," he said.

"Sit on the bed."

"What?"

"The bed. Sit. The one thing I know how to do is use physical therapy to ease the pain."

He dropped down onto the bed and she climbed behind him. Joshua felt Riley's hands on his neck. "I've got my credentials," she said as her fingers started to move slowly on his neck, pressing under the collar of his shirt, moving down to his shoulder, then back up to the line of his jaw. He closed his eyes as he felt the tension ease out of him.

"Tension gets everywhere," she said softly, her fingers working magic on him. "Even here," she said, and found a spot under his ear. "There." She rotated her fingers on the spot and the relaxation started to change. "Is that better?" she asked softly from somewhere close to his right ear.

"Much," he murmured.

Then her fingers moved down to his shoulders again, working under the collar of his shirt, skin against skin, and the relaxation evaporated. Each touch set his nerves on edge and when he closed his eyes, all he was aware of was her touch and her scent around him.

It startled him when she pulled back quickly, and said, "That's good, isn't it?"

He turned and she was scooting off the bed, gaining more distance from him. He watched her and when she got to his side to go out the door, he stood and reached out for her, catching her by her wrist and pulling her around to face him.

Riley couldn't move. She didn't want to move. She felt surrounded by Joshua, by the man and his world, and she wanted desperately to snuggle into it and to pull it around her and never leave it. She wanted just as desperately to be closer to him, to feel him against her, to feel his touch on her. And when his hand moved, slipping to the nape of her neck, gently pulling her toward him, she went willingly.

She ached for more and twined her arms around his neck, arching into him, feeling him respond, lifting her high into his arms. They fell together onto his bed, into the coolness of the comforter, and twisted until he was over her, his lips burning a path to her throat, then finding the wildly beating pulse there.

His hands were on her, tugging at her shirt, lifting

the cotton. His hand pressed to her middle. Heat against heat, skin against skin, and she shuddered as his hand moved higher. As his lips ravished hers, his hand found her breast, the thin lace covering hardly a barrier at all, then it, too, was gone, and he found her nakedness. The moan came from deep inside her as his lips left hers and trailed down to take the place of his hand on her bare breast.

She buried her hands in his hair, throwing her head back, lost in the sensation. The connection was everything to her, the feel of him with her, that sense of not being alone. She needed more. Fumbling with his shirt, tugging at the buttons, finally opening the soft cotton, her hands found his chest. His heart hammered under her palms and she tasted his skin with her lips. The salty heat and the sleekness.

His hand moved lower on her stomach, tucking his fingers into the waistband of her jeans and the button popped open. The palm of his hand pressed against her lower stomach and he shifted, angling to be able to skim his hand up over her stomach, up to her breasts, then down again, lower this time, pushing aside the stiff denim of her jeans.

She pushed at his shirt, shoving it back and off his shoulders, wanting skin to skin, with no barriers, and she finally succeeded. Her breasts pressed to his naked chest and she could hear her own soft moans echoing around her as his hand found her center, cupping her, pushing against her, making her hips lift to the contact.

His head went lower, his lips skimming over her exposed stomach, trailing fire with each kiss, and she lay there, unable to do anything but absorb the pleasure his touch was giving her. Everything was here and now, nothing from any other time or place intruded, and she was lost in a sea of anticipation and aching need. Then the world shifted and she realized that a phone was ringing somewhere off in the distance, that Joshua was pushing up and back, muttering a harsh curse as he swung away from her.

She was alone on the bed, him standing over her, and she could see the way his desire was barely contained by his jeans. He made no effort to hide it when he uttered, "The phone. It could be Dad or an emergency at the station."

No, it could be reality, she thought, and sank back weakly into the mussed bedding. Reality. She didn't know if she hated the caller or if she should thank him. She turned from Joshua, rolling onto her side to the edge of the bed, and sat up. She heard Joshua leaving the room and grabbed her shirt, pulling it around her, then fumbled to redo her bra.

She hated the desperation she felt, the need that literally made her spirit and body ache. Joshua couldn't be the answer to any of her needs and she wouldn't be a throw-away affair. She knew that if something really got started between them, she couldn't leave. It would kill her to leave. Stopping had been a good thing, for both of them. No matter how much it hurt.

By the time Joshua got back to his old bedroom, Riley was dressed and putting on her boots. Her hair had come loose from the band and it fell in a riot around her face as she bent to do up the laces. He could taste her on his lips and his hands ached from the memory of how she felt. She didn't look at him as she stood and said, "Trouble?"

"No, it was Todd. The jail's clear," he said, pushing his shirttail back into his Levi's and doing up his zipper. She still didn't look at him. He was stunned at the strength of his need for her, and felt fragmented and confused. He wanted to reach out and pull her back to him, to say, "To hell with the world," but he couldn't. No more than he could face the fact that he'd felt things this past week that he hadn't ever thought possible again. In one week, one person had turned his life on its ear.

"Tell me something," she said softly.

He shrugged, uneasy at the brightness in her eyes and the unsteadiness in her voice. "What?"

"If I told you right now that I'm guilty, that I really did all the things you think I did, would you want me here with you now?" She bit her lip before saying, "Would you want me at all?"

He stared at her, words tumbling through him, but none would come out. He couldn't say whether or not it would matter. He couldn't take his eyes off her pale skin, and her hands clenched so tightly in front of her that her knuckles were bloodless.

"Are you guilty?" he heard himself asking, and kicked himself when she closed her eyes for a long moment, then opened them, but didn't look back at him. Instead she moved past him quickly, bumping his arm in the process as she muttered tightly, "Take me back to jail."

He hurried after her and caught up to her in the living room where she'd just grabbed her jacket. "That's it? I didn't say what you wanted me to say, so that's it?" he asked, his jaw so tight it ached.

She twisted, shaking out her jacket and muttering, "Damn it, damn it," then finally pushed her arm through one sleeve and twisted to put the other one in. Her arm missed the sleeve and she jabbed at it again before he went over to help.

Once she was dressed, she headed for the door so fast she was bordering on a jog. "Riley!" he called as he went after her.

She opened the door before she turned back to him. "What?"

He came closer, pulling on his own jacket as he moved. They stood face-to-face, and he heard himself saying, "So, did you steal the car?"

The color drained out of her face and he had the horrible thought she might faint again, but she didn't. She actually lifted her chin slightly, met his eyes without blinking and said, "If you still don't know, it doesn't matter at all, does it?" She turned from him before her words died and went out into the cold night.

The ride back to the jail was painfully quiet, with Riley sitting as far as she could from him, literally pressing against the door. He didn't look at her, but stared straight ahead after leaving the ranch, and by the time he pulled into the parking area at the jail, he was finding it hard to breathe. They made their way back inside the station.

"Hey," Todd called from the front desk. "Every-thing's settled. I escorted the troublemakers out of town myself, and even cleaned up the cells."

"Great," Joshua said with a wave of his hand, and kept going after Riley.

She'd disappeared through the door to the cell area and by the time he got there, she was in her cell, turning to reach for the door. She met his gaze and deliberately pulled the cell door shut with a hard clank. Then she turned and crossed to the cot, stripped off her jacket, stepped out of her boots and grabbed the blankets and pillows stacked on the cot.

She took her load to the corner and tossed it onto the cement floor. She dropped down on top of the pile, pushing at the pillows, then with a sigh, clutched one of the pillows to her middle and leaned back against the bars. She closed her eyes. He moved closer, staring down at her through the bars, and finally said, "What do you want from me?"

She sighed again as she clutched the pillow more tightly to her breast. "I don't know. Maybe for you to believe me," she all but whispered.

Oh, God, he felt sick. He knew how short he'd fallen and how impossible it was for him to say, "I believe in you." He looked at the gentle line of her chin, the sweep of her throat as she put her head back against the bars, the pulse that worked wildly just below her ear, and the dark arcs of her lashes against her pale cheeks. All he had to do was believe her. But he was a cop, and he needed proof, even though deep in his heart he knew she couldn't be guilty.

"If I can't, that's that?"

"That's that," she echoed softly, and turned away from him, pulling the pillow up to stuff it between her head and the bars.

He lifted his hand, compelled to touch her hair through the bars, but he didn't. Instead he turned and left the cell area.

He almost ran into Todd in the other room, but kept walking, snapping over his shoulder, "What now?" as he headed for the office.

Todd caught up with him at the door to the office. "Just thought you'd want to know that nothing's come in on the inmate. No calls, no faxes." Joshua stopped in the doorway and turned to the other man.

"Nothing at all?"

Todd shook his head. "I thought you should be the one to tell her."

Joshua didn't want to tell Riley, either. "Let's wait," he said, and went into his office.

"Are you staying for the night shift?" Todd asked from the doorway.

He would have any other time, but he shook his head. "No, I'm just getting some papers, making a few calls, then I'm gone."

"You going to the practice for the pageant?"

"No, I'll head home," he said, and Todd left.

In five minutes Joshua had made his calls and finished his work. He had no other reason to stay. He went to his car and didn't realize where he was headed until he'd reached the entrance to the inn. His mind was going in circles, and he had to figure out what was happening to him.

Jack had been wrong. Being with Riley wasn't just about lust. He cared. He never thought he would again, but he did. He'd thought that most of his life was dead and gone, that J.J. was all he'd need now to be happy.

But now that Riley was in his life, he felt things he could barely deal with. It was total insanity, mixed with need, and something else. Something he couldn't name.

He'd known Riley for less than a week. He'd known Sarah for a year before he'd been sure of his feelings for her. This didn't happen. It didn't make sense, and he hated when things didn't make sense. Before turning off the road and heading to the inn, he changed his mind and continued driving. Jack had his own demons to wrestle with now, and Jack wouldn't understand. No one would.

He and Jack were similar but different in a number of ways. Jack was at a crossroads in his life, a place of evaluation, sorting things out, but Jack had never been in love. He'd joked he'd been "in lust" many times, a joke that had gone on for years. So he'd never had love and lost it, as Joshua had, and he'd never found it again, the way Joshua could.

As that thought hit him, his foot pressed on the brake and he felt the big car slide for a moment, the brake pedal pulsate, then steady as the tires gained traction. Finding love again? In less than a week? With a stranger? No, that wasn't possible.

Joshua drove more slowly, staring straight ahead. Love. He'd lost love in the blink of an eye, in a split second it had been gone. He gripped the steering wheel. Could it come again in a split second? Could it come in such an improbable way? He looked at himself in the rearview mirror, at his pained expression. Could something that unexpected and tenuous be real? Could he believe in something so sudden and stunning? Could he believe in Riley?

He turned the car around, headed back to the town, passing the inn without a glance. He kept going, then turned onto a side street, parked behind a beat-up pickup and got out into the frigid night. He headed toward the Briar. Once inside, Joshua saw a sign over the bar, framed by holly leaves, that read Beware The Christmas Punch. It's Got A Punch!

Pudge was behind the bar, obviously sober and obviously not terribly happy. Joshua shrugged out of his jacket, hung it over a stool and took the next one. "Beer," he said to Pudge, and the skinny man filled a mug with draft, then put it in front of him.

"About the other night, Joshua…" Pudge said.

Joshua brushed him off. "Forget it."

"I appreciate it, I really do. My life's in the sewer and if I drink, it goes even deeper. Marriage is driving me crazy…again." He frowned intently. "Man, I don't get women."

"Join the club," Joshua said, taking a sip of his beer.

Pudge put one hand flat on the bar top, balling a towel in the other. "Speaking of women, Wes was telling me about that pretty young prisoner you've got over at the station. Figured she was the one you showed up with the other night when I was bombed. Couldn't rightly remember what she looked like, but Wes was telling me that she's still saying she's innocent and she sleeps on the floor. She's got everyone running around like chickens with their heads cut off. Even got curtains in her cell."

Joshua stared into his beer, then took a long drink.

Pudge leaned closer, not getting the hint that Joshua

didn't want to talk about Riley. "Women, they'll do you in." He shook his head with despair. "It's their karma or something. Do in men. That's it. They do in men." He held up one hand, showing four of his fingers. "Me, I've been done in four times. Four times." He rubbed the towel in his hand on the bar with a vengeance. "Damn karma. Damn women. We're better off alone."

Joshua stared at himself in the smoky mirrors behind the bar. Better off alone? He finished his beer and pushed the empty mug toward Pudge. "More," he said, feeling more alone than he had in a very long time.

Pudge brought it back to him and leaned forward, his elbows resting on the bar top. "Hey, you got something going on you want to talk about?"

Joshua shrugged, staring hard into his beer. "I thought I understood my life, then it all went crazy."

"You know, I'm real sorry about what happened to you, Joshua."

He looked at Pudge and for a split second he thought the man was talking about Riley, then he realized that he was referring to Sarah. It stunned him that the uncertainty with Riley was the first thing he'd thought about. He drank more beer and put the mug down with a muffled thud as "White Christmas" came over the jukebox.

"You want to talk? I owe you, and this place ain't exactly jumping tonight. I got time."

The bartender slash shrink. Joshua shrugged, finished the last of his beer, waited for Pudge to get him another one, then said, "I've got plenty of time." And he needed to talk to someone.

Chapter Thirteen

Riley was surprised that she'd actually slept, even if
it had been almost dawn before she'd fallen asleep.
She woke with a start, on the floor in a tangle of blankets and pillows, and couldn't figure out what had
awakened her. Then she knew.

She heard someone running, and turned in time to see
J.J. burst through the security door at full speed, barely
stopping at the bars. One hand grabbed at the cold steel
and the other one clutched a sheet of paper. "Riley for-
got," she said, pushing the paper through the bars toward
Riley.

The drawing. The family. Riley took it, smoothed
it out and forced a smile for J.J. "Thanks for bringing
it to me."

J.J. grinned at her. "Santa's comin' soon," she said
earnestly.

"Just another week or so."

J.J. frowned. "Him's real busy. Mamaw says."

"Yes, I guess he is," Riley said, pushing herself to
her feet and crossing to the other picture taped to her
wall. She tore off a piece of the tape that held the first

drawing and used it to fasten the second drawing alongside it. Then she turned and saw Gen standing beside J.J.

"Where did Joshua go last night?" Gen asked.

Riley moved closer to the woman and child. "He dropped me off here, then left." She hadn't heard him come back, but he could have. "Why?"

"He never came home, and now Wes says he didn't spend the night here." Gen frowned. "I just wondered if you knew where he'd spent the night?"

Riley felt heat in her cheeks. "No, I sure don't."

"I see," was all Gen said, and seemed disappointed, as if Riley should know exactly where Joshua was.

"Maybe he's at the inn with Jack."

Gen's face brightened. "You know, I didn't think of that. He could be." She left but J.J. stayed and grinned at Riley.

"Know what?" she asked.

Riley crossed to crouch in front of her through the bars. "No, what?"

"Santa lives here."

Riley mocked surprise. "Where's his house?"

"It's magic. Just disappears," she said in a low voice.

"Oh, I see, magic."

"Huh," she said, nodding her head. "Magic."

"I thought Santa lived at the North Pole."

J.J. nodded again. "Mamaw says it's cold there."

"Smart woman," Riley murmured, and, hearing footsteps approaching, saw Gen coming through the door.

"J.J., come on. We have to get going." Gen addressed Riley. "Josh isn't at the inn, but Jack heard he got drunk at Pudge's last night and he ended up at the hotel. Annie let him use her extra room." Gen frowned. "Joshua never gets drunk."

Riley wished she'd been drunk last night. Maybe she wouldn't have stopped what was happening and maybe she would have at least had a few hours alone with Joshua. But really all she wanted was for him to believe she was innocent. "At least he's okay."

"For now," Gen said, taking J.J. by the hand. "I'll be back later on for your shower. And I'll make sure they bring in your breakfast."

"Thanks," she said, and waved to J.J. "If you find Santa, you let me know, okay?"

J.J. nodded with a smile and left with Gen.

Riley crossed to the cot and sank onto it, staring at the two pictures. She was startled when someone spoke to her. "Miss Shaw?"

She turned to see Todd at the cell door. "Oh, yes?"

He actually smiled at her, a first in all the time she'd known him. "I've finally got good news, ma'am."

She jumped to her feet and hurried to the cell door. "What?"

"The owner of the car, Mr. Wise?" She nodded and he continued. "Well, it seems that he reported the car stolen when his wife, Mindy Sullivan, took it. They were in the middle of a really nasty divorce and he was getting even with her, I guess. Anyway, she's the one who had her attorney hire you to drive it to San Diego. The wife didn't know about the car being reported stolen. So Chicago said that there is no case, and to offer you their apologies." He stood even more erect and all but saluted her. "You're free to go, ma'am."

She felt light-headed with relief and held on to the bars for support. "Are you sure?"

"Absolutely sure." He motioned behind him. "I just got the papers from Chicago. A real mix-up." He motioned to the cell. "If you want to get your things together, I'm having Rollie bring the BMW over." He turned, hit the code for the door and she tugged the door open. "In ten minutes, you can be on your way."

She wanted to ask whether or not Joshua knew, but she didn't. "Well," she said on a heavy sigh. "It was a mistake."

He frowned slightly, obviously expecting her to be jumping up and down with joy, or be totally furious. But she just felt numb. "A mistake by two people who supposedly loved each other enough to get married, then hated each other. Now they seem to be on a second honeymoon in Mexico." He shook his head. "That's why no one could find the owner. No one knew where they were, let alone that they were together." He frowned at her again. "Are you all right, ma'am?"

She tried to smile, but imagined that the smile looked more like a grimace. It just didn't feel right. "I'm just shocked," she said truthfully.

"I know you can lose your faith in the way this system works, but it does work, eventually," he said earnestly.

"Yes, it does," she breathed.

"I'll go and check on the car."

"Officer Todd?" she said when he turned to leave. He looked back at her.

"Ma'am?"

She didn't know what she wanted, so she just said, "I'll be right out."

He left and she methodically went about gathering her stuff. She put the pillows and blankets back on the cot, slipped on her jacket and boots, then picked up her duffel and turned to leave. But she stopped. The pictures J.J. had made hung on the wall. She hesitated, then crossed and took them down. She folded them carefully, then put them in her duffel and left the cell.

It felt strange walking out of the cell area without an escort. No, it felt strange knowing she was leaving, even though it was what she'd wanted all along. But for a stunning moment, she felt as if she were leaving home. The thought almost made her laugh out loud. Her home was a jail? That made as much sense as the feeling of walking away from something incredibly important.

No one was in the squad room, but she saw movement in Joshua's office. She headed in that direction, but stopped in the open door when she saw it was Officer Todd. He was standing by the desk, reading over some papers in his hand, then looked up at her.

"Rollie stopped to gas up the BMW." He reached for a manila envelope and her purse. "Here's your things," he said, and held them out to her. She dropped her bag and jacket and took the purse and envelope. She looked through the contents.

Once she'd verified nothing was missing he handed her a pen and a piece of paper, and said, "Sign and date this."

Once she'd done as he'd asked, Officer Todd said,

"Miss Shaw, we really do regret this inconvenience to you."

Inconvenience? That was such a mild word compared to what had happened to her in less than a week. "It's over," she murmured.

Todd came around the desk. "Rollie will be at the side entrance in a few minutes. Why don't you wait in here and I'll let you know when he shows up?"

He left her alone and she looked around. For one brief moment she thought of staying until Joshua showed up. She could show him the papers from Chicago and see his face before she walked away. Or maybe she wanted to stay, to see if things could be different. Could they be different? She closed her eyes, feeling a flicker of hope, something she'd seldom felt in her life. Maybe, if they could talk, if she could explain things, maybe…

She heard footsteps and she turned, hoping that it was Joshua. But it wasn't. Charlie stepped into the office and smiled at her. "Rollie's got the car in the side lot," he said. "I'd like to say it was good to meet you, but I know you don't feel that way at all. So, I'll just say, I'm really sorry for all of this, but glad that we never booked you. Joshua was right about that. Less mess and no paper trail. Best of luck to you and have a safe trip to San Diego."

"Thank you," she said, and he hesitated, then turned and left.

She stood there, not moving. Hoping. Then a soft ringing accompanied by a humming sound caught her attention. She saw a sheet of paper being fed out of the fax machine. Normally she wouldn't have paid it any attention, but she saw her name printed in letters right at the top of the page. "Re: Riley Shaw."

Moving closer to the machine, she read the printed copy below the title and all hope disappeared. It was from Harvey Sills, the P.I. from Chicago. The body of the fax was printed in block letters, easily readable for anyone. "Juvenile records, sealed, but arresting officer in two cases, gave overview. F.Y.I..." Then there was a starkly simple summary of her past sins. From her first arrest at thirteen to this near arrest for auto theft.

Nausea rose in her throat with vengeance. She glanced at the door, then at the fax. She didn't want Joshua to see her past contained on one page of cheap fax paper, so she reached for it and stuck it in the pocket of her jacket. Then she walked out the door and left the Silver Creek jail without a backward glance.

JOSHUA WAS HUNG OVER big-time. His head hurt. His bones hurt and his skin hurt. When Annie came up to his small attic room at the hotel, even her knock on the door hurt. He sat up in his rumpled clothes, wished he had a gallon of ice water, and mumbled, "What?"

"Gen said to get home, and Todd called from the station."

"Thanks," he muttered, and forced himself to get up and stand, however rocky that venture became.

"Can I get you anything?" Annie called through the door.

A life, he thought numbly, but said, "Water, coffee and a shower."

"Water and coffee will be waiting for you downstairs. The shower's one floor down and empty right now."

He looked at a small clock on the side table. Nine o'clock.

"Thanks," he called, and headed for the door. By the time he had it open, Annie was disappearing down the stairs.

"Plenty of towels on the side cupboard," she said with an airy wave.

He went after her, slowly, trying very hard not to jar his head with each step he took. Fifteen minutes later Joshua was out of the shower, in the same clothes, but he felt much better. He drank half a pitcher of ice water and took the foam cup of coffee she had left alongside the frosty pitcher. "How much do I owe you?" he asked, narrowing his eyes at the harsh glare of daylight all around him.

"Nothing. You saved my skin a few times," Annie said with a grin. "Let's just say we're even."

He started to nod, but stopped and said, "Okay, for now."

"Todd called again, sounded pretty hyped about something."

"What's going on?"

"Todd said he needed to talk to you about Miss Shaw."

His head seemed to clench with more pain at the mention of Riley's name and he narrowed his eyes. "What about her?"

She looked oddly reticent to say anything else. "You need to talk to him right away."

"Annie, what did he tell you?"

"Okay, okay." She sighed. "Just don't tell him I told you, because he told me not to and I don't want him to—"

"Annie," he cut in abruptly. "What?"

"Seems you were holding her for nothing. That car wasn't stolen at all, and Todd signed her out and let her go."

Joshua stared at her. "What?"

"Todd said he signed her out. Rollie brought the car to the station and—"

Before she could finish, Joshua grabbed the coffee and ran for the door. He hurried out into the cold, felt it hit his head with a searing jab, then ducked into the wind and hurried down the street toward the jail. That was when he saw her—at least, he saw the big black BMW. Even from a distance he could make out the Illinois plates. He broke into a run, called out to her, but the car never stopped. It headed south and away from Silver Creek.

He made it to the jail, hurried inside and confronted Todd. "What's going on?"

"Miss Shaw just left." Joshua listened while Todd told him a story that matched Riley's claims to a T, and he knew how horribly wrong he'd been.

"Did Sills get the information for you?"

"No, we didn't hear from him. Detective Gagne faxed it in. If I'd checked your faxes sooner, I would have seen it an hour earlier, at least."

"And she's just gone?"

"Yeah, she got the car, signed off on her possessions, then left." He studied Joshua intently. "Listen, if you're worried about her suing, I wouldn't be."

Suing? He couldn't care less about that. All he knew was that he didn't want Riley to have left with no goodbye. Without trying to figure out why that was so important, he left the office. Realizing his car was still parked at Pudge's, he said, "I'll take the extra cruiser," to no one in particular and left.

Within minutes, he was on the road and could see the black BMW just ahead of him. He hit the lights, then the siren and felt heady relief when the brake lights flashed and the car pulled onto the side of the road where the snowplows had cut out a clearing.

He got out quickly into the cold air and strode ahead to the driver's side of the BMW. The tinted window was rolled down and it felt like déjà vu all over again. Riley driving, him pulling her over, her looking out at him, but this time there was no anger. Her eyes were wide and overly bright.

She stared up at him, not speaking, and he hunkered down, grabbing the window frame with both hands as he crouched. She looked at his hands on the black metal, then back at him. "Officer Todd told me I could go," she said, her voice so low he could barely hear her.

"I know, but I need…" What did he need? He needed her. That was it. But he said, "I need to talk to you."

She bit her bottom lip. "Why?"

A car went past, the air stirring around him. "It's important," he said, then looked to his right when another car went past, so close he felt the vibrations of the engine against his back. "But not here."

He wasn't sure if he expected her to just take off, or what, but he was genuinely taken aback when she said, "Yes, I guess we do need to talk."

"Good, good," he murmured.

"Where?" she asked.

He shook his head. "I know a place. Just follow me, okay?"

She nodded, then he stood and she rolled up the tinted window. He went back to the cruiser, then drove out on the road and past her. He held his breath until she pulled out behind him, keeping her distance, but definitely following.

He went south for a few miles, then saw the turn he was looking for. He hadn't been to the place for years, probably since he was twenty or so, on a trip back here after his first year of college. He slowed on the side road where the snow was piled on the sides and barely made enough clearance for one car. He drove slowly, constantly glancing in his rearview mirror. Then he saw what he was looking for and signaled to let Riley know he was turning right.

He turned into a narrow drive and pulled over to park. Riley did the same with the BMW. He got out, and Riley followed.

He led the way along the path to the front porch of the cozy, snow-covered house. He took the steps two at a time and reached above the door to find the key. It wasn't there and for a minute he thought he'd have to break in. Although he'd done that more than a few times when he was younger, he happened to see the glint of metal at the far corner of the high doorjamb. He reached for it and felt the cold key.

"Come on inside," he said as he pushed the key into the lock and swung the door back.

He moved aside to allow Riley to enter, then went

behind her and closed the door. She stopped just inside and looked around. "What is this place?" she asked.

"It's a cabin Jack's grandfather bought and never parted with. A lot of the old-timers around here kept their original places." He looked around the main room. It hadn't changed much in all the years he'd been coming here.

The walls were a bit dingy, needed a new coat of paint and the braided rugs that laid over peg-and-groove flooring were faded and worn in spots. The furniture was pleasant, nothing fancy, tweed and very old leather with a couch and chairs facing the fireplace in the back wall. He started for the hearth. "I'll get a fire going," he said, and crouched by the wood stacked to the right of the firebox.

Jack had used several logs and hadn't restocked, which wasn't like him at all. The ashes in the fireplace were still in the vague shape of those logs, at least until Joshua picked up the poker and prodded at the remnants in the hearth. Then they broke apart and turned to nothing but ashes. He set about building a fire, touched a match to the kindling and finally stood and turned.

Riley was standing by the door, still in her jacket, not moving. She was watching him silently. He motioned to the couch. "It'll be warm soon. Take off your jacket and sit."

"What did you want to talk about?" she asked, not making a move at all.

"Please, sit down," he said, shrugging out of his jacket and tossing it onto the hearth.

She hesitated, then came toward him. "Joshua, you don't need to apologize or worry that I'll sue you or anyone in Silver Creek."

"I wasn't going to apologize," he said honestly. "And I don't give a damn if you sue every person in Silver Creek."

She stopped. "Then what—"

"I didn't want you to leave. I got drunk last night at Pudge's." He grimaced. "Dead drunk."

"Gen said you ended up at the hotel."

"Yeah, I ended up there. Do you want to know why?"

"No, and it's not my business."

He went closer. "Isn't it?" He was so close he heard her take each breath. "I think it is."

She looked down at her hands, clutched together in front of her. "Why?"

He reached out, cupping her chin softly and lifting her head until he was staring into her eyes. "Why? Because I hated what happened last night. I hated my rigid attitude, and I hated leaving you in that cell. I knew you didn't belong there."

Her tongue darted out and touched her pale lips. "No, you didn't, not until the papers came in this morning."

He shook his head. "They just confirmed what I knew." His thumb moved over her silky, warm skin. "What I think I always knew," he breathed, his whole body responding to that simple touch.

RILEY EXHALED and knew that she shouldn't have come here at all. And she shouldn't want to stay. But she did. With all her heart, she wanted to stay. But she couldn't. The paper in her pocket had shown her that she had to get out of here. She didn't even know a man like Joshua existed days ago, but right now she could admit that if she was different, if what she was didn't matter, he could be her world.

He was even closer now, his hand moving to the nape of her neck, and in that moment she knew that she wanted one more thing. She wanted this time with him. Just to be with him, to hold him and to be held, and to love him. Then she'd leave. But she'd take this with her. She went to him, pressing her face into his chest, standing very still, afraid to move in case he let her go and this was truly over and done.

"What are we going to do?" she whispered.

He laughed, a low, rough sound in his chest. "I've got a good idea what I'd like to do," he murmured.

She closed her eyes tightly and balled his shirt in her hands. "Are you sure?" she asked.

He ran a hand over her back, then cupped the nape of her neck and pressed his lips to her hair. "Very sure. Very sure." His lips trailed to her temples, then her eyes, then her mouth.

She'd thought if this could happen, she wanted it to last forever, but the instant his lips found hers, she had a frantic need to know him, to be one with him. Kisses rained down on her and his hands were pulling aside her clothes, pushing at the cotton, tugging the jeans down, until she was naked except for her panties and bra. She felt his hands on her bare skin and she wanted to feel him, too. She tugged at his shirt, freeing it from his Levi's, then found the snap at his waistband. She undid it with fumbling hands and instantly felt his desire pressing against the rough material.

She tried to get her fingers to work, to undo the zipper, but it was useless. She was shaking too hard. Then Joshua had her in his arms and was carrying her. They tumbled onto the bed in the space beyond the fireplace, onto cold linen and a soft, down comforter, tangling together, arms and legs entwined, bodies pressing to each other and kisses edged with desperation.

She tasted him, felt his muscles in his back, his heart against her lips when she kissed his chest, then his hands were on her and she lay back, arching to his touch, moaning softly as he found one sensitive spot after another. Her bra was gone and his hand found her breasts. His lips took the place of his hand and she cried out softly, overwhelmed by the sensations that flared through her.

His hand moved lower, exploring, testing, and her panties were pushed down and were gone. He touched her, finding her center and again she arched toward him, gasping at the feelings that soared through her. She cried out when he left her, and she looked up, found him standing over her by the bed, and in the flickering light from the fireplace, she saw him take off the last barrier.

With his jeans and boxers removed, he was even more magnificent than she'd thought. His eyes held hers for a long, aching second, then she reached out to him. "Please," she whispered, and he came to her. He trembled when she found him, when she circled his strength, then he was over her, braced by his hands at either side of her shoulders. He was touching her, testing her, and she lifted her legs, circling his hips. She felt him against her. Grabbing his shoulders, she pulled him down with her legs.

He entered her in one movement, deeply and completely and they both lay there, their rapid breathing rough and unsteady. His face buried in her neck, his lips nipping her skin, trailing fire on her, as they moved in harmony. The partial withdrawal, then the thrust, as white-hot passion took over. Both of them touched and tasted, then moved and met with each thrust, going higher and higher.

Riley felt herself holding on to Joshua, afraid to let go in case she shattered into a million pieces. Then the climax came and she knew that she wasn't fragmenting, she was becoming one, feeling him as if he were a part of her, thrilling at the completion she found with him. The home that was Joshua. Her place in the world. For that one shining moment he was hers and she was his. They were together. Totally. And that was all that mattered.

Chapter Fourteen

Joshua felt Riley fall into a deep sleep and he held her to him. He inhaled the scent of her skin, felt the heat of her breath brushing his chest and the feel of her leg resting heavily over his thighs. He waited for some flashing moment of guilt, maybe sadness, but it didn't come. It wasn't there. What was there instead was a sense of rightness, of being where he was supposed to be.

It wasn't that Sarah hadn't counted, that she was forgotten, but that he'd slipped into another part of his life. A good part, with Riley. He pressed a kiss to her forehead and tasted the damp saltiness of her skin. He relished the taste, then felt her stir. The instant she moved against him, his body responded. Then she twisted to look up at him. They had to talk, but it could wait till tomorrow—he wanted to share all the tomorrows with her.

He dipped his head and kissed her again, then felt her hand stroke over him, lower, and she found that he wasn't done. He wasn't sated by a long shot. She shifted higher, and she was over him, straddling him, her hair falling forward in a veil around her face. "One more time?" she asked on a rough whisper.

One more time? No, time after time, after time. But he simply touched her cheek, then brushed at her hair. She moved higher and he spanned her waist, helping to lift her, then lower her slowly onto him. She arched back with a gasp that echoed his own when he entered her. She leaned forward, her hair brushing his skin, her lips hungry for his, and she started to move.

They matched each other thrust for thrust, over and over again, going higher and higher, and in that moment when they both cried out, Joshua knew that his new life had begun. Here and now. With Riley. A new life.

RILEY HELD ON to Joshua for as long as she could, feeling him fall asleep against her, his arm around her, his breath hot on her skin. She wasn't sure she'd be able to survive what she had to do, but she knew she couldn't stay. She gathered all her courage and slipped out of his hold, letting him shift and settle before she quietly got out of the bed into the cold air of the cabin. She didn't turn to look at him; she couldn't and still leave, and hurried in silence to get her clothes on.

Finally she was ready. Taking the paper from her pocket, she placed it on a table by the couch, anchoring it with the edge of a lamp, then found a pen and wrote a note at the bottom. "This is what I wanted to tell you. This is why I'm leaving. Have a wonderful, wonderful life." Then she signed it with a single *R*.

She quietly crossed the room, grabbed the doorknob, then did what she knew she shouldn't do. She looked back at Joshua in the bed. He was on his side, turned away from her, his bare shoulder a soft curve in the dim light. She could see each breath he took, then he sighed, and settled. And her heart broke.

She turned quickly away, went out the door into the early evening and closed the barrier as quietly as she could. Settling into the BMW, Riley sat there but didn't turn it on. Then, turning the key partway, she put the car in neutral and rolled it back and down the drive to the road. That's when she turned on the motor and the lights, and left.

She had her dream. For almost a week, she lived a dream. And all the bad things in that dream were forgotten because in the end she had experienced the best thing she'd ever known in her life. She drove back to the highway, tears threatening to push their way through. As she drove, she felt numb. But Riley was used to the pain, she expected it. To survive, she needed to embrace it.

While she drove, she willed herself to not think about Silver Creek or Joshua. And for more than half an hour she almost succeeded. When a police siren blared behind her, her hands jerked and the big car swerved slightly to the center line, then back into its lane. Looking in her rearview mirror, Riley saw a high SUV with interior warning lights.

"Damn it," she muttered, wishing she'd thought to bring a copy of the paperwork Officer Todd had at the station.

She pulled to the side, stopped, rolled down her window and waited. She couldn't see into the cruiser until the cop opened the door and his lights flashed on.

Only one cop, and as he got out she saw the silhouette of a tall, thin man in a bulky jacket and a hat pulled low. He came up to her window and hunkered down to look inside.

"License and registration," he said curtly, and stretched out a hand expectantly.

Her heart sank. They'd find out the truth after contacting the Silver Creek police, but that didn't matter. Nothing really mattered right now. She turned to get her license out of her wallet, then handed it to him. She watched him skim a flashlight over it, then he looked in at her again.

"Riley Shaw?"

"Yes. What's the problem? Why did you pull me over?"

He ignored her questions as he reached in, pushed across her to grab the keys in the ignition, and turn off the car before he jerked them out. "Stay right here," he ordered.

"Sir," she said quickly. "I need to explain to you—"

"Save it," he snapped, then turned and went back to his SUV. He got in, left his door open and she could see him speaking on his radio. Riley watched him in the rearview mirror.

"Come on," she muttered. "Just arrest me and get this over with."

He didn't move. He was reading something in the cruiser, and time dragged on. The cold was getting worse without the heater going and she couldn't even put up the automatic window without the keys. Just when she was ready to go back to explain things to him, he got out of the SUV. But he didn't come toward the BMW. Instead he looked down the road and Riley saw another squad car approaching them with its lights flashing.

Riley sank farther down in the seat and closed her eyes. She'd get through this. She'd leave. She almost jumped out of her skin when someone said her name at the window.

"Riley?"

She jerked around and saw Joshua standing there. The sight of him made her heart lurch. "What…what are you doing here?"

He pulled her door open, then motioned her to get out. "Getting you," he said.

She didn't expect him to reach in and grab her by her upper arm, then tug her out into the cold air. But he did, and she went with him. As they stood face-to-face, Joshua's hand still held firmly to her arm. He wasn't looking at her, but at the other cop. "I'll take the keys," he said, and held out his other hand. The man dropped the keys in Joshua's palm.

"Anything else?" the man asked, looking cautiously from Riley to Joshua.

"No, I can take it from here," he said.

The man touched his cap, then turned and left. Riley watched him get in his SUV and drive off.

"Okay, let's go back," Joshua said.

He mustn't have found the paper. But she couldn't. If she went back, she'd never leave. "No, I'm leaving," she said.

He let her go, but he stayed where he was. "You left. Why?"

Her legs felt like jelly and she moved back enough to use the car for support. "I had to," she breathed.

He exhaled heavily, his breath curling into the cold air. "I thought that you…that we had…" He pushed his hands deep into his jacket pockets and hunched his shoulders slightly. But he never looked away from her. "Okay, I know you're going to San Diego and you've got a great job waiting for you. I'm betting the guy who hired you to take this car there is going to give you a huge bonus. But…" His voice trailed off as his features tightened. "Riley, I'm an idiot. I should have told you a long time ago that I never thought you were guilty. Hell, I can't remember when I really did believe that you were. I should have told you."

The numbness was fading and she hated it. "So you found out I didn't steal the car and you're saying the right things?"

"No, it's not like that. I got drunk last night because I knew how much I'd hurt you. No, that's not true. I got drunk because I couldn't face the changes in me, the feelings that seemed wrong. But now, they're all that matter."

"Joshua, stop it. I can't stay here." Her voice was unsteady, but she couldn't change it. Not any more than she'd tell him she'd made love with him so that she'd have something to hold on to in this life when life got cold again. "Didn't you find the paper I left?"

He looked blank for a moment, then pulled his hand out of his pocket. He had it crushed in a ball in his hand. "This?"

She nodded. "Then you know what I am, what I did. Jack was right. I'm all wrong, this is all wrong. I have to leave. I'm not a part of this world, and I'm sure as heck not good enough for you, or for J.J. Sarah, she... You love her, and I'm not Sarah."

He shook his head. "Sarah..." He said her name so softly, she almost didn't hear it. "You're right, I loved her. I always will in some way, but she's part of a life that died when she did. This is my life now. This is what makes me feel alive, what makes me want to go on and love someone."

"What?" she asked, almost afraid to believe what she thought he'd said.

He looked at the crumpled paper in his hand, then opened it, smoothed it slightly, then very deliberately tore it into a thousand pieces. He looked right at her, then tossed the paper into the air, letting it go with the wind.

"Love, Riley Shaw. Love, unique and wonderful and something that feels as if it's given me life again. It's you." He didn't touch her. "You," he said hoarsely.

"I was arrested a lot...for a lot of things."

He shrugged, not looking shocked or impressed. "I told you I got arrested once. I never told you I took a snowmobile from Rollie's garage and crashed it into the new car of Pudge's second wife." He lifted one eyebrow. "I was tough. A real hoodlum, spent a night in jail and everything."

"Joshua, this isn't funny," she breathed.

He reached for her then, pulling her into his arms. "No, it's not funny. This is my life, and your life. And I want to spend them together." He moved back, one hand on her cheek, then brushing back her hair. "I can't live without you."

"What about the others? They'll be upset and angry and—"

"No, they won't. No matter what Jack or my dad or Gen or anyone in this town feels about me loving you, they only want what's best for me. And you're best for me." He kissed her quickly and fiercely, then pulled back. "Please, Riley Shaw, save me. Be with me. Let me love you forever?"

The tears were there now and they slid silently down her cheeks. She didn't care. "You love me?" she managed to whisper, still unable to believe it.

"Love seems like such an inadequate word for what I feel for you." He looked uncertain for a moment. "Could you love me…and J.J…and Gen…and Dad?"

She smiled, an easy expression for her. "I already love you so much, and J.J. and your family."

He lifted her into the air, into his arms and spun her around in the coldness of the night. As snow began to fall again, he looked into her face, and said, "Welcome home, Riley Shaw."

Epilogue

Two days before Christmas

RILEY STOOD in the tower suite at the inn at midnight, waiting for Joshua. When he came in to the room, his tux was half-off. His tie was gone, his shirt snaps undone, his jacket nowhere in sight. "Well, it's done," he said.

She watched him coming toward her. "It sure is."

He stood inches from her, but he didn't touch her. "Are you very sure about this?"

She had never been more sure of anything in her life. "Very sure," she whispered, then reached out to him. She was in his arms, holding him tightly. She still wasn't used to this. Being able to touch him whenever she wanted to. To make love wherever they wanted to, whenever they wanted to. To be with him and not standing behind bars, watching him. To have someone who loved her and who she loved. It was new and exciting and a bit frightening.

She loved Joshua with every atom of her being. "Thank you, thank you," she whispered.

"You're thanking me for marrying you?" he breathed against the side of her neck. "I should be thanking you for staying and letting me love you. It wasn't easy."

He eased back enough to start undoing the buttons on her white velvet dress. Gen had found it at a local store—a short, formfitting, cocktail-length gown that was sleeveless, with a long row of velvet-covered buttons running down the front. It was fancier than anything she'd ever worn before, and she hadn't been comfortable about buying it. But Gen had insisted. When she'd put it on this morning for the wedding, it was perfect.

One by one, Joshua undid the buttons, stopping occasionally to kiss her. Then he muttered, "Damn buttons. The guy who invented them should be shot."

Riley laughed, but the sound grew unsteady when Joshua tugged the dress down, then let it slide into a puddle at her feet. "Finally," he breathed, his hand cupping her breasts, but his eyes never left hers.

The phone rang and Joshua closed his eyes for a moment, then said, "Stay right here," and crossed to pick up the phone. "What?" He listened. "Thank you. Thank you. Sure, of course." And he hung up.

He came back to her. "Pudge. Says we can go there anytime and the drinks are on the house. And congratulations."

"Lovely man," she murmured, but the bar and drinks weren't on her mind when Joshua leaned close, wrapped his arms around her and undid the fastener on her bra. The lace fell down to join the dress and his touch was on her, skin on skin.

The phone rang again. "Let it ring," Joshua murmured, but when it kept ringing without going to voice mail, he'd finally had enough. He kissed her quickly, then went back to the phone. "Yes?" He frowned. "Sure, thanks. Yes, I do." He hung up. "Annie. She said to tell you that she wants to welcome you to Silver Creek."

He came back to her, but this time he didn't hesitate. He lifted her into his arms, leaving the dress and bra on the floor, and carried her to the upper level and into the main bedroom. Stone walls, a huge bed, a fireplace big enough to walk into, and the fragrance of wood smoke in the air, but she barely noticed any of it. All she saw was Joshua with her, in the bed, over her, smiling down at her. Then the phone rang again.

He rolled off of her, hit the pillow with the flat of his hand, then twisted to reach for the extension by the bed. "What?" He listened for a long moment, then said, "Great, great, great. Now lose this number." And he hung up.

He rolled back over to her, lifted himself up onto his elbow to look down at her. "That was Todd. The BMW got to San Diego fine. The owner wants to give you a bonus."

"We can use it," she said, reaching up to touch his lips with the tip of her finger. "It might get tough with me helping Gordie at the clinic. I know there won't be much money in it, but it'll be good. And you're going to have to figure out what you want to do, now that you're not going back to Atlanta. If you want to still work as a cop or if you want to—"

He pressed a forefinger to her lips to hush her.

"Riley, there's something I should have told you before, but it never came up."

She felt her heart lurch slightly. "Bad or good?"

The phone rang again and he uttered a rough expletive that she'd never heard him use before as he rolled back over to reach for it. "Yes?" He listened, didn't speak until a full minute must have gone past. "Thanks for that update." He listened. "Yes, and we love you all, too." With that he hit the disconnect button, but didn't put the receiver on the hook. Instead he stuffed it under the bank of pillows on the bed.

He stood, stripped off his tux and the rest of his clothes as he said, "That was Gen. J.J. fell asleep with her flower girl bouquet and a new picture she drew." She had a brief glimpse of him totally nude before he quickly came back to her and lay down, resting on his elbow to look down at her. "Dad's resting. Gen's working on the extra rooms for us, and it'll be ready in a week." They'd decided to live at the ranch for a while, as a family. His hand stroked her hair. "They all send their love."

God, she loved family. She just loved it, almost as much as she loved her husband. But she was still waiting for his answer to bad or good. "Now, is your confession good or bad?"

"Oh, it's good. I think, I hope, it is."

She was getting nervous. "Just tell me."

He brushed at her shoulder and swept his hand down to the curve of her hip, pulling her closer. "I'll make this short and relatively simple. You know Jack and I grew up together."

"You and Jack and Cain." Cain Stone was at the inn.

He'd been at the wedding briefly, but Riley had barely talked to him before he'd left. "If this is some sort of confession about something you did, then I don't want to hear if you burned down some place—"

He stopped her words with a quick kiss, then pulled back. "No arson, I promise. The land he inherited, it butts up against land that I own, part of my ranch." His hand stroked her hip lightly, then rested at her waist. "He wanted to build this place, develop it, and it made sense to purchase more land, so I went in with him. He did the active work, took care of things, and I went along for the ride since I was in Atlanta then."

She was confused. "What's the confession?"

"I'm a stockholder in Jack's company. Actually, co-CEO with him. I go to some board meetings and do some work for them, but I've stayed out of it for most of the time, been sort of a silent partner. But now I'm back here, I think I'll get more involved."

That was it? "You're going to work with Jack?"

He kissed her quickly. "Yes, I think I will. Since you're hooked up with Gordie at the clinic, for the physical therapy, I like the idea of staying around Silver Creek."

"Me, too," she sighed. The job offer from Gordie had come out of the blue, but it was perfect.

"Riley, you don't have to worry about money." He grimaced, as if he was going to say something very distasteful. "I've got money. A great amount of money, actually."

"Gen said that Sarah also had money."

"No. All of Sarah's money is in trust for J.J. until she turns twenty-one. I'm talking about my money."

He leaned toward her and she thought he was going to kiss her. But he didn't. He whispered in her ear and she couldn't believe what he'd just said.

"You mean, you have…" She swallowed. "How much money?"

He repeated it, out loud this time, and she bolted upright. "You're kidding, aren't you?"

He lay back in the pillows, smiling up at her. "No, I'm not. I can get the actual figures, but that's it, within a million or so."

"Within a million or so!" She reached for one of the plush pillows on the bed, pressed it over her face and screamed at the top of her lungs. She could hear him laughing, but she could barely comprehend what he'd told her. Then she let the pillow drop and exhaled in a rush. "Holy cow!" She grinned down at him. "Rich Joshua?"

He reached out to pull her back into his arms. "No, just very-much-in-love Joshua." He kissed her, long and deep. "And happy Joshua," he whispered, then kissed her again.

A pounding on the door jolted them and Joshua sat up and yelled, "What?"

A voice called, "Sir, your phone seems to be off the hook."

"Yes, it does, and it's going to stay off the hook," he said to Riley, but called, "It is, and it's staying that way."

"Yes, sir," the voice said, then was gone.

Riley grinned at Joshua, then gave herself to her husband. She loved him completely, and she wanted to show him how much. She felt her soul healing with each touch and each kiss. Finally, she had come home. Silver Creek and Joshua, were home. And when they lay in the darkness together, far into the night, she turned to him and whispered her own secret.

It didn't matter if he was rich or poor, a cop or a CEO, she simply loved him with all of her heart and soul, and she would love him forever. It was that simple...finally.

* * * * *

Look for the next story in Mary Anne Wilson's
RETURN TO SILVER CREEK *series,*
as the mysterious Cain Stone
reveals some secrets, later in 2005
from Harlequin American Romance.

Welcome to the world of American Romance!
Turn the page for excerpts
from our September 2005 titles.

We're sure you'll enjoy every one
of these books!

It's time for some BLOND JUSTICE!
DOWNTOWN DEBUTANTE is Kara Lennox's
second book in her series about three women
who were duped by the same con man
and vow to get revenge.
We know you're going to love
this fast-paced, humorous story!

Brenna Thompson drew herself deeper into the down comforter, trying to reclaim the blessed relief of sleep. But instead of drifting off again, she awoke with a jolt and smacked into hard reality. She was stranded in Cottonwood, Texas, without a dime to her name, her entire future hanging by a thread.

And someone was banging on her door at the Kountry Kozy Bed & Breakfast.

Wearing only a teddy, she slid out of bed and stumbled to the door. "I told you to take the key," she said grumpily, opening the door, expecting to see Cindy, her new roommate. "What time is it, any—" She stopped as her bleary eyes struggled to focus. Standing in the hallway was a broad-shouldered man in a dark suit, a blindingly white shirt and a shimmering blue silk tie. He was a foot taller than Brenna's own five-foot-three, and she had to strain her neck to meet his cool, blue-eyed gaze.

In a purely instinctual gesture, she slammed the door closed. My God, she was almost naked. A stranger in a suit had seen her almost naked. Her whole body flushed, then broke out in goose bumps.

The knock came again, louder this time.

"Uh, just a minute!" She didn't have a robe. She wasn't a robe-wearing sort of person. But she spied one belonging to Sonya, her other roommate, lying at the foot of her bed. The white silk garment trailed the floor, the sleeves hanging almost to Brenna's fingertips—Sonya was tall—but at least it covered her, sort of.

Taking a deep breath, she opened the door again. "Yes?"

Still there. Still just as tall, just as imposing, just as handsome. Not her type, she thought quickly. But there was a certain commanding presence about this stranger that made her stomach swoop and her palms itch.

"Brenna Thompson?"

Deep voice. It made all her hair follicles stand at attention.

"Yes, that's me." He didn't smile, and a frisson of alarm zapped through her. "Is something wrong? Oh, my God, did something happen to someone in my family?"

He hesitated. "No. I'm Special Agent Heath Packer with the FBI. This is Special Agent Pete LaJolla."

Brenna saw a second man lurking in the shadows. He stepped closer and grunted a greeting. Both men looked as if they expected to enter.

Brenna glanced over her shoulder. The room was a complete wreck. Every available surface was covered with clothes and girly stuff, not to mention baby things belonging to Cindy's little boy. Even fastidious Sonya's bed was unmade. Sonya was used to servants doing that sort of thing for her.

Special Agent No. 1 didn't wait for her consent. He eased past her into the room, his observant gaze taking everything in.

"If you'd given me some warning, I could have tidied up," she groused, pulling the robe more tightly around her. She hadn't realized how thin the fabric was.

Mustering her manners, Brenna cleared off a cosmetics case and a pair of shoes from the room's only chair. "Here, sit down. You're making me nervous. And...Agent LaJolla, was it?" She brushed some clothes off Sonya's twin bed. LaJolla nodded and sat gingerly on the bed while Brenna retreated to her own bed. She sat cross-legged on it, drawing the covers over her legs both for warmth and modesty.

"I assume you know why we're here," Packer said.

*If you enjoyed Penny McCusker's
first book for American Romance,
MAD ABOUT MAX (April 2005),
you'll be happy to hear that her second book,
NOAH AND THE STORK, has arrived!
And if you haven't read her before,
you'll be delighted by
Penny's warmhearted humor in this
charming story set in
the town of Erskine, Montana.*

Men were generally a pain in the neck, Janey Walters thought, but there were times when they came in handy. Like when your house needed a paint job, or your kitchen floor needed refinishing or your car was being powered by what sounded like a drunk tap dancer with a thirst for motor oil.

Or when you woke in the middle of the night, alone and aching for something that went way beyond physical, into realms best left to Hallmark and American Greetings. Whoever wrote those cards managed to say everything about love in a line or two. Janey didn't even like to think about the subject anymore. Thinking about it made her yearn, yearning made her hopeful, and hope, considering her track record with the opposite sex, was a waste of energy.

She set her paintbrush on top of the can and climbed to her feet. She'd been sitting on the front porch for the past hour, slapping paint on the railings, wondering if the petty violence of it might help exorcise the sense of futility that had settled over her of late. All she'd managed to do was polka-dot everything in the vicinity—the lawn and rosebushes, the porch floor and herself—which only made more work for her and did nothing to solve the real problems.

And boy, did she have problems. No more than any other single mom who lived in a house that was a century old, with barely enough money to keep up with what absolutely had to be fixed, never mind preventative maintenance. And thankfully, Jessie was a normal nine-year-old girl—at least she seemed well-adjusted, despite the fact that her father had never been, and probably would never be, a part of her life.

It only seemed worse to Janey now that her best friend had gotten married. But then, Sara had been waiting for six years for Max to figure out he loved her, and Janey would never have wished for a different outcome. She and Sara still worked together, and talked nearly every day, so it wasn't as if anything had really changed in Janey's life. It just felt...emptier somehow.

She put both hands on the small of her aching back and stretched, letting her head fall back and breathed deeply, in and out, until she felt some of the frustration and loneliness begin to fade away.

"Now there's a sight for sore eyes."

Janey gasped, straightening so fast she all but gave herself whiplash. That voice... Heat moved through her, but the cold chill that snaked down her spine won hands down. It couldn't be him, she told herself. He couldn't simply show up at her house with no warning, no time to prepare.

"The best scenery in town was always on this street."

She peeked over her shoulder, and the snappy comebacks she was famous for deserted her. So did the unsnappy comebacks and all the questions she should've been asking. She couldn't have strung a coherent sentence together if the moment had come with subtitles. She was too busy staring at the man standing on the other side of her wrought-iron fence.

His voice had changed some; it was deeper, with a gravelly edge that seemed to rasp along her nerve endings. But there was no mistaking that face, not when it had haunted her memories—good and bad—for more than a decade. "Noah Bryant," Janey muttered, giving him a nice, slow once-over.

Tina Leonard continues her popular
COWBOYS BY THE DOZEN series
with CROCKETT'S SEDUCTION.
These books are wonderfully entertaining
and exciting. If you've never read
Tina Leonard, you're in for a treat.
After all, who can resist a cowboy—
let alone twelve of them!
Meet the brothers of Malfunction Junction
and let the roundup of those
Jefferson bad boys begin!

Even now, at his brother Bandera's wedding, Crockett Jefferson wondered if Valentine Cakes—the mother of his brother Last's child—realized how much time he spent staring at her. His deepest, darkest secret was that she evoked fantasies in his mind, fantasies of the two of them—

"Well, that's that," his eldest brother, Mason, said to Hawk and Jellyfish, the amateur detectives and family friends who'd come to the Malfunction Junction ranch to deliver news about Maverick Jefferson, the Jefferson brothers' missing father.

Before he heard anything else, Crockett once again found his eyes glued to Valentine and her tiny daughter, Annette. Watching her was a habit he didn't want to give up, no matter how much family drama flowed around him.

Hawk looked at Mason. "Do you want to know what we learned about your father before or after you eat your piece of wedding cake?"

Crockett sighed, and took a last look at the fiery little redhead as he heard the pronouncement about

Maverick. She was holding her daughter and a box of heart-shaped petits fours she'd made for Bandera's wedding reception. She smiled at him, her pretty blues eyes encouraging, her mouth bowing sweetly, and his heart turned over. With regret he looked away.

She could never know how he felt about her.

He really didn't *want* to feel the way he did about the mother of his brother's child. So, to get away from the temptation to keep staring, he followed Hawk, Jellyfish and Mason under a tree so they could talk.

"We were able to confirm that Maverick was in Alaska for a very long time," Hawk said.

Crockett thought Mason surely had to be feeling the same excitement and relief that filled him; finally some trace of Maverick had been found.

"But we felt it was important to come back and tell you the news, then let you decide what more you need to learn," Hawk said.

Crockett felt a deep tug in his chest. Now they would hold a family council to decide what to do. It was good they'd found out now, since all the brothers were at the ranch for the annual Fourth of July gathering and Bandera's wedding.

Now that so many of the Jefferson brothers had married and moved away, Mason wanted to hold a family reunion at least twice a year—Christmas in the winter and Fourth of July in the summer. Christmas was a natural choice, but Independence Day was a time when the pond was warm enough for the children to swim, Mason had said. But Crockett knew his request really had nothing to do with pond water. Mason just wanted the brothers and their families together, on the so-called Malfunction Junction ranch, their home.

Crockett had to admit there was something to the power of family bonding as he turned to again watch Valentine with her tiny daughter.

*HIS WEDDING, by Muriel Jensen,
is Muriel's last book in the saga of
the Abbotts, a northeastern U.S. family
whose wealth and privilege could not
shield them from the harsher realities of life,
including a kidnapping.
At last the mystery of the kidnapping
is solved—by the missing Abigail herself,
with the help of Brian Girard,
himself an Abbott child who is soon
planning his wedding!*

Brian Girard sat on the top porch step of his shop at just after 6:00 a.m., drinking a cup of coffee while reading the *Losthampton Leader*. The ham-and-cheese bagel he'd bought tasted like sawdust when he saw the front-page article about Janet Grant-Abbott's move to Losthampton, and he'd thrown the bagel into the garbage.

"Long-lost heiress home again," said the caption under a photo of Janet that must have been taken on her return from Los Angeles.

From the small plane visible some distance behind her, the setting was obviously the airport. Her hair was short and fluffy, and she was squinting against the sun.

At a glance she resembled any other young woman on a casual afternoon. It was the second look that made you realize she was someone special. Her good breeding showed in the tilt of her head and the set of her shoulders; the intellect in her eyes elevated a simple prettiness to fascinating beauty.

The article revealed all the known details of her kidnap, the Abbott family's position in the world of business, her brothers' accomplishments, then her own history as a successful stockbroker.

It went on to say that her adopted sister had come to Losthampton thinking she might be the missing Abbott sister, Abigail, but that a DNA test had proven she wasn't. And that had brought Janet onto the scene.

He was just about to give the reporter credit for a job not-too-badly done, when he got to the part about himself:

"Brian Girard, the illegitimate son of Susannah Steward-Abbott, Nathan Abbott's first wife, and Corbin Girard, the Abbotts' neighbor, has been welcomed into the bosom of the family." It continued in praise of their generosity, considering that Corbin Girard was responsible for the fire in their home and the vandalism to the business Brian owned. It explained in detail that Brian had been legally disowned for defecting to the Abbott camp by giving the Abbotts information that stopped them from making a business deal they would have regretted. Brian has no idea how the paper had gotten that information, unless one of the family had told them.

Annoyed, he threw the newspaper in the trash, on top of the bagel, and strode, coffee cup in hand, down his dock. The two dozen boats he'd worked so hard to repair bobbed at the ends of their lines, a testament to his determination to start over at something he enjoyed.

The refinished shop was restocked with the old standbys people came in for day after day, plus a few new gourmet products, a line of sophisticated souvenirs and shirts and hats with his logo on them—a rowboat with a grocery bag in the bow—visible proof of his spirit to survive in the face of his father's continued hatred.

He could fight all the roadblocks in his path, he thought, gazing out at the sun rising to embroider the water with light, but how could he fight the truth? No matter what he did, he would always be the son of a woman who'd thrown away her husband and other two sons like so much outdated material, and of a man who'd rejected him since the day he was born.

The sorry fact was that Brian couldn't fight it. He could do his best to be honest and honorable, but he would never inspire a favorable newspaper article. Every time his name came up, it would be as the son of his reprehensible parents.

He didn't know what to do about it.

Then again, Janet Grant-Abbott wasn't sure what to do, either.

AMERICAN *Romance*®

Fatherhood: what really defines a man.

It's the one thing all women admire in a man—
a willingness to be responsible for a child and
to care for that child with tenderness and love.

NOAH AND THE STORK
by Penny McCusker
September 2005

Noah Bryant's job has brought him back to
Erskine, Montana—and the girl he once loved. It's
no surprise that Janey Walters is all grown up now
with a daughter of her own. But Noah gets the shock
of his life when he finds out he's Jessie's father….

BREAKFAST WITH SANTA
by Pamela Browning
November 2005

Tom Collyer unwillingly agrees to fill in as Santa
at the annual Farish, Texas, Breakfast with Santa
pancake fest. He's not surprised by the children's
requests for the newest toys. He is surprised when
one young boy asks for something Tom—or
Santa—can't promise to deliver: a live-in father.

Available wherever Harlequin Books are sold.

www.eHarlequin.com   HARFH0805

HARLEQUIN®

AMERICAN *Romance*®

Catch the latest story
in the bestselling miniseries
by

Tina Leonard

Cowboys BY
THE DOZEN!

Artist, rancher and bull rider Crockett Jefferson
has always been a man of strong passions. So
when he finds himself thinking passionately
about the one woman he can't have—
Valentine Cakes, the mother of his brother's
child—this sensitive cowboy knows
he's in trouble!

CROCKETT'S SEDUCTION

Harlequin American Romance #1083

Available September 2005

If you enjoyed what you just read,
then we've got an offer you can't resist!

Take 2 bestselling love stories FREE!
Plus get a FREE surprise gift!

Clip this page and mail it to Harlequin Reader Service®

IN U.S.A.	IN CANADA
3010 Walden Ave.	P.O. Box 609
P.O. Box 1867	Fort Erie, Ontario
Buffalo, N.Y. 14240-1867	L2A 5X3

YES! Please send me 2 free Harlequin American Romance® novels and my free surprise gift. After receiving them, if I don't wish to receive anymore, I can return the shipping statement marked cancel. If I don't cancel, I will receive 4 brand-new novels every month, before they're available in stores! In the U.S.A., bill me at the bargain price of $4.24 plus 25¢ shipping & handling per book and applicable sales tax, if any*. In Canada, bill me at the bargain price of $4.99 plus 25¢ shipping & handling per book and applicable taxes**. That's the complete price and a savings of at least 10% off the cover prices—what a great deal! I understand that accepting the 2 free books and gift places me under no obligation ever to buy any books. I can always return a shipment and cancel at any time. Even if I never buy another book from Harlequin, the 2 free books and gift are mine to keep forever.

154 HDN DZ7S
354 HDN DZ7T

Name	(PLEASE PRINT)	
Address	Apt.#	
City	State/Prov.	Zip/Postal Code

Not valid to current Harlequin American Romance® subscribers.

Want to try two free books from another series?
Call 1-800-873-8635 or visit www.morefreebooks.com.

* Terms and prices subject to change without notice. Sales tax applicable in N.Y.
** Canadian residents will be charged applicable provincial taxes and GST.
   All orders subject to approval. Offer limited to one per household.
   ® are registered trademarks owned and used by the trademark owner and or its licensee.

AMER04R   ©2004 Harlequin Enterprises Limited

e HARLEQUIN.com

The Ultimate Destination for Women's Fiction

Your favorite authors are just a click away
at www.eHarlequin.com!

- Take a sneak peek at the covers and
  read summaries of **Upcoming Books**

- Choose from over 600
  author **profiles!**

- Chat with your favorite authors
  on our **message boards.**

- Are you an author in the making?
  Get advice from published authors
  in **The Inside Scoop!**

**Learn about your favorite authors
in a fun, interactive setting—
visit www.eHarlequin.com today!**

INTAUTH04R

HARLEQUIN *Super*ROMANCE®

Big Girls Don't Cry

by
Brenda Novak

Harlequin Superromance #1296
On sale September 2005

Critically acclaimed novelist
Brenda Novak brings you another
memorable and emotionally engaging
story. Come home to Dundee, Idaho—
or come and visit, if you haven't
been there before!

On sale in September
wherever Harlequin books are sold.

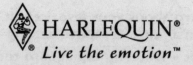

HARLEQUIN®
Live the emotion™

www.eHarlequin.com   HSRBNBGDC

HARLEQUIN *Super*ROMANCE®

HARLEQUIN SUPERROMANCE
TURNS 25!

You're invited to join in the celebration…

**Look for this special anthology
with stories from three
favorite Superromance authors**

25 YEARS

(Harlequin Superromance #1297)

Tara Taylor Quinn
Margot Early
Janice Macdonald

*On sale September 2005
wherever Harlequin books are sold.*

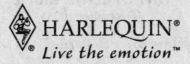

HARLEQUIN®
Live the emotion™

www.eHarlequin.com   HSR25YEARS0805

HARLEQUIN®

AMERICAN *Romance*®

BLOND JUSTICE

Betrayed…and betting on each other.

DOWNTOWN DEBUTANTE
by Kara Lennox
(September 2005)

All jewelry designer Brenna Thompson wants
is to get back the priceless gems stolen by
her thieving ex-fiancé. FBI agent Heath Packer
thinks he can help—but he has an ulterior
motive, one he can't share with her. Being
with Brenna makes Heath appreciate life…
but what will she say when she learns the
truth about his investigation?

Also look for:
HOMETOWN HONEY
(May 2005)

OUT OF TOWN BRIDE
(December 2005)

Available wherever Harlequin Books are sold.

www.eHarlequin.com　　　　HARBJ0805